As a River

SION DAYSON

For my family, blood and chosen

ISBN: 978-1-938841-10-1

Dayson, Sion

As a River / Dayson

CONTENTS

Part One: Past and Present

Part Two: Present and Future

As a River

It should have been harder for a young black boy to slip undetected from a small Southern town. To hitch rides, travel back roads, set sail for who knows where.

And yet he did. A boy, green to the world, has power. A boy, freshly cut, can move unseen. Greer might have thought demons had come to claim him at the time, but in fact, he had angels too.

Now sixteen years later, at age thirty-two, Greer took his first steps back into Bannen. On the exterior, very little had changed since he had last seen it. He, on the other hand, had doubled in age. Expanded exponentially in experience.

Greer wouldn't say he had left Bannen without a trace. He had sent intermittent postcards, though nothing more than signs he was alive. He knew that some of them arrived because he received a few notes in return, *forgive me* or *come home* scrawled on scraps of unlined paper. He didn't expect more words than that. Why would he? He read these things as he sat amidst foreign people, under different skies.

It wasn't Elizabeth who told him she was sick. Greer had always thought of her as sick, but this was something different.

Reverend Smith wrote to him about his mother in an unsure hand. Greer pictured it, the illness, and it wasn't too far from the image he'd always carried of her—that of a tumor resting too close to her heart.

*　　　*　　　*

Greer bought the bike on a whim. It was a rusty old thing resting against Bannen's worn bus station when he pulled in, a *FOR SALE* sign hanging on the handlebars. He sussed out who it belonged to within the day and the bike was his before nightfall. His purchase had to do with finding a new way to travel these streets from a former life. To move faster, to pick up speed if he needed. He would not be pulled back in.

"Well, I'll be," people would say, people like Wilson, who Greer hadn't even been sure would still be around. An idle thought among the more serious. But there he was, alive and kicking.

That first day back Wilson looked him up and down. "Greer, we 'bout thought you was a ghost."

"And how do you know I'm not?" Greer said, only half joking.

Greer's mother, used to ghosts, gave him what seemed at first a genuine smile, a rare thing, until it turned into something of a grimace, tears rolling down her face.

"I'm sorry, I'm sorry," she said like an incantation.

"Mama, it's ok," he said, putting his arms around this woman so fragile he could think of nothing but bones.

"I'm so glad you're back, baby. Everyone always leaves me. I'm so glad you're back."

Part One:
Past and Present

ONE

(1977)

Ceiley grew up hearing of her own immaculate conception. Kids in the schoolyard would ask her who her father was, goading her to say God. She never did, but that didn't stop their taunts. Stories thick as kudzu in that town. Everyone knew about her mother.

The town, Bannen, was a small one in middle Georgia, made of dirt roads and modest homes; the air heavy, ground loamy. Oak trees and chickenfeed, the Cherokee Rose that offered a second flowering in the fall if lucky; these were things you saw from the front steps of Wilson's General. People said they could smell Sicama River, better known as Snake Creek, from half a mile away—about as far as anyone ever went. On warm summer evenings, a remote train whistle would sound, a reminder of other places in the distance. But mainly, like the train's call, a town beyond Bannen was a reality fleeting, then gone.

Ceiley hadn't heard the whistle, was still sitting at the dinner table, moving the lima beans across her plate into pleasing geometric patterns. Trapezoids, hexagons, equilateral triangles. Her mother clanged dishes behind her, as if a chorus could be made of pots and pans. When the tap stopped running, one final gurgling sound issuing from the drain, Ceiley heard Esse's familiar huff. She didn't need to turn around to know her mother was looking critically at the back of her head, finding fault with her unraveling cornrows, or the unsatisfactory way she slumped her shoulders. Ceiley ignored these silent assessments and waited for Esse to move to the closet for the broom.

"Mama," she said, "Sheila asked me to come over to her house after school tomorrow."

"Who's Sheila?" Esse asked, starting to sweep near the stove.

"Someone in my class. You know, one of Mrs. Stevens'. She's nice. It would be nice to go. She lives over on Cedar." A vegetal rhombus, perpendicular lines intersecting.

"You know we have plans."

"Mama, really," Ceiley said, "do I have to go to church with you *every* day?"

"Child, what kind of question is that? The Lord is with us every day. *He* always shows up."

Ceiley shifted her beans into straight lines, the flanks of a regiment. "Mama," she would try to put it in her mother's language, "I've already prayed for everything—peace, love, health, humility. Not much more to do."

"Humility?" Esse said, the broom's rapid scratches on the worn linoleum floor coming to a halt. "Girl, you like looking up words in that big dictionary of yours, I think you need to look that one up again. You prayed for every living being already? There are more creatures on this earth than days you'll be alive, you could start with that."

Ceiley dropped her fork on the plate, the bang louder than she expected.

"Damn it, Mama, I'm fifteen. You never let me do anything," she said, the words flying from her mouth before she could stop them.

"There will be no swearing in this house," Esse said, coming toward her, gripping the broom's handle so tight Ceiley imagined splinters of wood suddenly shooting forth from her mother's fisted hand.

"Nothing's allowed in this house!" she said, pushing her chair away. She ran out the back door and circled around the small house, muttering what her mother would consider further indecencies. In her agitated state, she collided with a man on a bicycle.

"Are you all right?" the man asked, jumping off, laying the bike on its side. He reached a hand out to Ceiley, who was splayed on the ground, and helped lift her up. Ceiley dusted her clothes off, dazed, unable to meet the man's eye.

Seeing that she was fine, the man laughed. "Kid, maybe you should look up, see where you're going."

The front door flung open. "Girl, don't think you can run out like that," Esse shouted. She looked liable to say a lot more, but seeing the man standing there stopped her short. She looked at him for a few long moments, then nodded slightly, as if she had just decided something in her head. "Greer?"

"Is that you, Esse? Been a long time."

She nodded again. "Didn't know you were back."

Ceiley looked at her mother in wonder, speaking to a stranger like he wasn't.

"Yeah, just got in. Came to check on my mother. How has she seemed to you?"

"She don't get out of the house, can't say that I seen her much."

"Of course," he said, as if this were helpful information. Then, after a pause, "and how are you?"

Ceiley could see he was looking at her mom, squinting a little which made tiny lines appear by the sides of his eyes, but for one exquisite moment her own breath caught imagining that he was asking her.

Beautiful.

Now that she allowed herself to study him, she took in just how beautiful he was—soft-looking skin the color of cocoa, a wide carriage, a warm, if hesitant smile.

"Fine, just fine," Esse was saying, waving her hand as if brushing the question away.

He nodded, then looked at Ceiley. She flushed, having those deep, kind eyes trained on her, something flickering behind them.

Before she could figure out what, her mom went and ruined things as usual.

"Well," she said, grabbing Ceiley's arm, "we'd best be going."

"Ok," Greer said. "We'll be seeing you."

Ceiley tried to wriggle free from Esse's grip—"Mama, I was going somewhere"—but Esse flashed her get-in-the-house gaze.

Still, Ceiley stole one last glance at the man, this Greer her mother had called him.

"Who was that, Mama?" she asked as soon as the front door clanged behind them, too curious to even fear her mother's reprisal.

"Just a man. A man who left Bannen," she said. Ceiley felt her mother's look grow hot. "Don't you get any ideas," she said.

And what was that supposed to mean?

*   *   *

Greer looked around his old room. It was almost eerie; everything appeared just as he'd left it. Not a single book out of place, the wooden desk still wobbly, its right leg too short. The finish on the one dresser seemed dull as ever, the shelf above bare. The bed was made; that was the only change.

Of course, Greer didn't notice this at first. You expect a bed to be made when you enter a room. But after setting down his suitcase and taking it all in, letting the strange weight of return settle, he realized this one detail didn't match the memory. He had left that night in such a hurry. Would he have thought to straighten the sheets? Plump the pillows? No. He had fled in a fury.

Greer opened his suitcase and started unpacking his few belongings: clothes, compass, diary. He had learned to travel light. Still, his possessions seemed to take up a disproportionate amount of space. Had his room always been this small? It seemed he could barely fit. Then again, he'd always felt too big for this house. This house, small and silent and still.

Greer picked up the discreet black pouch that had almost gotten buried in the corner of his suitcase. He held it for a moment. He didn't need to take out its contents to know everything about it. He'd memorized its shape long ago. Caroline's necklace like a chain binding him to the past in a way he'd rather forget. Yet he'd never been able to let it go.

As he lay down that first night back, he wondered how many days his mother had waited before making his bed. Or had she done it right away? When she smoothed out the sheets, had she imagined sixteen years in between?

Greer got up again, too restless to sleep. He went to the bookshelf pushed against the far wall. So many times he'd read late into the night as a means of escape—it had all started here. He scanned the titles, most of them familiar, except a small group at the end. He'd never had a chance to really look at the last shipment he'd received before leaving. He remembered how his mother had always insisted on getting to those boxes of books first—and how life changed irrevocably the one time she didn't.

Greer pulled a book off the shelf, flipped absently through the pages before replacing it. He ran his finger over the spines, stopped at another book, the largest tome on the shelf. *War and Peace*. Well that about summed it up, didn't it?

Greer flipped right to the end of the book, as if the answer to it all could be found that easily. Something fell to the floor as he did. He leaned over and picked it up, a faded black and white photograph, the left corner severely bent. He unfolded it; the extreme crease sliced the photo with a thick white line. The picture must have been tucked in the book's pages for years.

He looked at the photo for a long time. It was disconcerting, but hypnotic somehow. Two white babies stared back at him. In the picture they held hands. He studied each tiny face, identical, their little mouths, their small ears mirroring each other.

He turned the photo over, found an inscription written in a right-leaning script he'd seen just once before: *Daniel and Caroline, 1943*.

Greer turned the photo over again. Which one was she? He jammed the photo back into the book and returned it to the shelf. But he changed his mind almost immediately and picked it up again. He walked to the closet and threw the book with the photo toward the back.

He flopped onto the bed again. He still couldn't believe he was back in Bannen. He must have known that one day he'd return, but he sure didn't feel ready. Reminders would be everywhere.

He closed his eyes tight, though sleep was nowhere in sight. Maybe, he thought, this was what his mother had felt when she'd found his room empty, realized he was gone: disbelief, yet with the unspoken knowledge that eventually it all catches up. It always does.

*   *   *

Ceiley never got to sleep in late, but it bothered her most on Sundays. Her mama's clattering wake-up call was unceremonious enough, but to then have to pile into a scratchy polyester dress and crowd into worn pews with the rest of East Bannen seemed further insult. Getting on toward summer, too, the torture only increased. Sweat seeping from every pore, the itchy polyester rubbing against her skin. While the preacher went on and on about brimstone and hellfire, she wanted to know: could it really be any worse than this?

At least she'd convinced her mother to let her quit the children's choir this year—not that she could claim that as a victory entirely on her own. Everyone in the congregation heard that she couldn't stay on key. The kids in school made even more fun of her for it—"Squealy Ceiley" they'd whisper when the teacher called her name.

Ceiley surveyed the congregation now, taking in the sea of fans flapping before all the same familiar faces. The fans provided some relief, sure, but she sometimes wondered if people weren't just pushing the hot air around that way. Waving some flimsy piece of paper didn't exactly cool down the inside of a broiler.

She wasn't concerned with the normal conditions this Sunday, however. No, today Ceiley scanned the hall looking for the stranger. She turned her head back to face front again, disappointed when she didn't see him. Not that she should be surprised. Miss Elizabeth never came to church, so why would he? How did some people get out of it, though?

Greer.

Gorgeous, golden, glorious, grand…She ran through as many words as she could think of that described him starting with the letter "G." She still couldn't get over how this fully formed perfect being had just dropped into Bannen, as if from the sky.

Reverend Smith was talking about the Exodus from Egypt, but Ceiley's mind was stuck on Greer—his smooth skin, that mysterious smile…

"Girl, pay attention," Esse said, shaking her arm.

It had taken the duet debacle when her voice had broken at just the wrong moment before Esse finally allowed Ceiley to step down from the choir. Though trying to sing was one less embarrassment, it meant she was back at her mother's side during services with all the hushing and jabbing elbows that came along with that position.

Ceiley opened her hymnal, but she couldn't focus at all on the words. She felt hot, but it wasn't because of the stuffy old church anymore, but because of these new, wandering thoughts. Were these the bad thoughts her mama had always warned her about? What was this new sensation causing her to tingle all over?

Everyone was clapping and hollering now, raising their arms to the music. This part wasn't so bad, though she'd always wondered what people were getting so excited about.

Just catching sight of Greer, though, could send her own mind and body into convulsions now. Her mama wouldn't like it one bit, but she could finally relate to the phrase "moved by the spirit." Only the spirit had nothing to do with God above, but a very real man who now lived across the street. Amen.

*   *   *

Elizabeth cooked simple meals, said she wasn't used to fixing anything for anyone else anymore. Greer could see how tired she was, how slowly she moved. He took over for her by the second day.

"Don't worry about it, Mama. I'm here to take care of you," he said, guiding her to a chair in the kitchen. "Maybe it's funny," he said, "seeing a man cook?"

"Never saw a man cook, no," she said.

Greer stirred the gravy. "Not that I always eat well," he said, trying to make conversation. "You can get used to eating some strange stuff out there."

"Is that right?"

She didn't sound too curious. Greer sighed. Even after all these years, she still had little to say.

"Maybe you're tired," he said. "Here, this will give you some strength." He set a plate in front of her, then fixed one for himself.

He sat down across from her. They ate in silence.

"Is it all right?" he asked finally.

"I can't stop looking at you, that's all," she said.

"Yeah, it's been a long time."

"Yes, too long, baby, too long."

He felt it creeping up. That old feeling of guilt. "You can understand I had to go."

"People gotta go sometimes," she said.

"Well, yeah, I did." And you were a part of it, he wanted to say.

The meat was too tough, but neither of them mentioned it. They tried to soften it with the gravy.

"So we're going to see the doctor."

"Oh, don't worry about that," she said.

"Don't worry? That's why I'm here," he said.

"We can talk about it later."

"Oh. Right," he said. "Later." He needed a cigarette.

Greer sat there while Elizabeth finished eating the mashed potatoes, pushed the peas around on her plate. She kept coughing. It sounded like it hurt.

"Well, we do have things to talk about," he said. "Don't we?"

Elizabeth didn't say anything. Greer tapped his finger against the table. After a few minutes, he noticed another sound. It had seemed just background noise before, but now the leaky faucet sounded explosive, each water drop hitting the sink like a liquid bomb.

"Got to do something about that," he said, getting up from the table.

"There's always been a problem with the plumbing here," she said.

Greer turned on the tap. Water sprayed from the faucet's head. "Got any tools laying around?" he said. "Probably needs a new washer, too."

"I don't have anything," she said.

"I'll go to Wilson's when he opens up tomorrow." How had she managed by herself all these years? He couldn't help wondering.

"Well, I'm going to take a bath," Elizabeth said.

"Ok, Mama. Need anything?"

"I'm fine, baby." She plodded off down the hall. He heard the water running a few minutes later.

Greer cleared the dishes from the table. Soaked the pan and washed the rest. He went out to smoke a cigarette on the porch, saw Esse's daughter across the way. He'd almost run her down the other day, she'd come barreling out of the house so fast. Strange, he had last seen Esse Phillips as a little girl younger than her own daughter was now. Time had passed here, even if the town appeared the same.

Riding in on the bus, he'd watched the landscape change. From that famous red clay—hard as iron, the color of blood—to the Tifton soil of Bannen, fertile, but a muddier brown. He felt himself move from iron resistance to a muddle of emotions. This place, like the invisible barrier segregating it into East and West, hadn't lost its power to shake him.

He looked out at the street, still unpaved, still untouched, and wondered if the dirt still transformed into rivers of mud after a hard rain. It must.

He turned his attention back to his cigarette, tried to concentrate on just the soothing inhalations and exhalations of deep smoke. Only a few days back and already he felt suffocated? Who knew how long he'd be here? He took a long drag, finally starting to feel his muscles relax a little when he heard Elizabeth's muffled voice. He opened the door and called in, "Everything all right?"

"Baby," she said, distressed.

Greer stubbed out his cigarette and ran into the house. As he made his way down the hall, he saw water starting to flow from the bathroom.

"Jesus. Mama?"

When he reached the bathroom, the visceral scene stopped him short. But it wasn't just the overflowing tub. His mother, naked, knelt on hands and knees, futilely attempting to turn off the tap. He tried to avert his eyes, but the surging water forced him into action.

"The handle broke off. I can't stop it," she said.

"Damn, why didn't you just take the plug out of the drain?" he asked, stooping down.

"I don't know. I wasn't thinking."

Greer pulled the stopper from the drain, then twisted the metal stump, all that was left of the faucet's handle. The water finally ceased.

"Like a goddamned flood," he muttered to himself. Then, more gently, he reached for Elizabeth's bathrobe and handed it to her as he helped her up.

"I'll get the mop." He turned away, as much to cover his awkwardness as for her privacy.

"I'll do it, baby. It was my fault."

"No, let me," he said. "Just go on and rest, Mama."

"I'm sorry, baby."

He cleaned up the mess, almost as meditation, while his mother changed into dry clothes. There's a lot that needs fixing around here, he thought.

THE FLOOD

(1944-1945)

Morning dew on the dogwoods, the maple trees, the shortleaf pines—at this time of year they could almost hear the moisture on branches crystallize into ice. The fresh chill blanketed East Bannen, but people still milled in the streets rather than stay cooped up inside. Wind blew through the cracks of their unheated clapboard houses; little warmth could be found in thin wooden walls anyway.

Miss Elizabeth, however, had gone into hiding. The whole town missed her at Sunday services, she the star singer. No one else in the choir could match her perfect soprano; there was no filling the void.

Elizabeth had not only shut her mouth, but shut down completely. Silent save the sobs that continued unabated for the near three weeks since Major's body was pulled from Snake Creek, she'd been unable to shake the cold ever since emerging from the dark water. She felt as if she were still drenched, her garments dragging her down, heavy with wet weight.

Clayton Major Michaels wasn't even from Bannen, a migrant come for the advent of the sweet potato harvest, but Reverend Smith had carried him down Main Street nonetheless, as a kind of warning to others of what might happen to lovers who dared to consort outside the confines of marriage, much less the confines of Bannen's town limit.

She hadn't joined the procession when they'd found him, but could feel when it passed her window, a shudder running down her spine. As they had marched by, the town shifted its gaze from the bloated body of this intimate stranger of hers to the sad façade of her shuttered house. Nothing stirred.

She didn't know what became of Major's body, where that horrible parade had ended. The preacher could have dumped him at the fork of the road, or neighbors might have seen fit to bury him with care under the red clay now hard from winter's approach, but the story for her had already stopped; suspended at the river, forever the grave and memorial, where before it had been the site of their love, fast and deep.

Steady, one of the local drunks, the most poetic, claimed to have seen Miss Elizabeth stumble home barefoot in the dead of night with silver pebbles in her hair and liquid jewels adorning her body, inert swaddling clutched to her breast, eyes shining wild like a swooping screech owl's. No one paid his ravings any mind, but it was the most they could piece together of why their knocks on her door were met only with grunts, how for several days running she refused to come out. She hovered in the kitchen, staring blankly at the damp pile scrunched tight in the middle of the table.

She couldn't stay locked up for all that time without leaving eventually though; she still worked for the Thomases. The church ladies and the unemployed boys, they all would have dragged her out if she had ceased heading towards Highway 75 each morning at dawn for the five-mile hike down to where the Thomas' driver picked her up. These were lean times, and no one had any right to decline an honest day's pay, no matter the circumstance. Whether being at the white man's beck and call was honest would later become a subject of public discussion here, but as yet, these were only private whispers behind closed doors.

And at that job, Elizabeth never spoke but was spoken to. Her silence in those heavy weeks of the drowning's aftermath appeared unremarkable as she lifted toilet seats to clean and peeled potatoes for mashing. And in that large, icy house there were times when she had need to run to the nearest alcove to unleash the cries lodged in her chest, that lump sometimes hard as coal, then dissolving into something liquid, torrential.

And on that one day she had snuck into the man of the house's personal study to seek solace and he had found her there, scolded and reprimanded, then somehow, as the brown room spun, she found herself gazing up at white lights and him on top of her.

She felt Mr. Thomas' heat rising off of him, his clammy hands hike up her skirt. She stared at the ceiling, a stark unadorned expanse, like the vast emptiness she now carried inside. All around the room stood tall, somber bookcases. She imagined them tumbling forward, all of them at once, a cascade of books to bruise and bury her.

Anything to bury her, she suddenly wished. Yes, to his crushing weight. As if from far away, from some surprise store of the subconscious, she heard herself murmur not, "Stop," but rather assent. *Flatten me into the floorboards, grind me into dust.*

Dust to dust. Ashes to ashes.

It continued like this—for days, for weeks, time's meaning evaporating—she submitting, sublimating her sorrow in the nearest warm place; that the closest one within reach should be Jeff Thomas might have seemed risky, but for her, this was no real danger, this land of salt—the taste of him in her mouth, the sodium of her tears. The *oh-ohs* sounded like *no-nos*, garbled, like underwater, filling ears, eyes, brain. Filling her heart.

Submerging it. *My baby splashes, my baby dashes, my baby has the prettiest eyelashes…* Major, his improvised songs, like the way he made love to her. On the spot. And now she, lying there under him, this other him, this white skin, unable to swim she sank trying to forget. And sometimes the shame of wanting to feel good because it hurt so bad would carry her far away like unremitting waves, like the ones that took Clayton Major, open and swallow, that river swallowed him whole. And like then, and like now, Elizabeth screamed, cried. River all over her face. Clawed, crawled, found and lost the shore.

Each time afterwards, she would cup her hand with water from the large basin in the bathroom and wash between her legs, then return to cleaning, broom or mop or rag in hand. The damp cotton of her underwear rubbing against her always reminded her, though. *Never again*, she would tell herself, but like clockwork, when he came looking for her, she repeated the same shameful scene.

"I thought I'd died," she'd say when her breath returned.

"You're all right, everything's fine," he'd say, not realizing she was disappointed she hadn't. He didn't understand that these little deaths of hers were tied intimately to her open wound. That he was not her lover, or her aggressor, or anything at all to her, for that matter. He held no position in her heart.

Since Major's death, nothing lessened her careening sadness. Not wailing or crying, the pounding of fists. So she ceased the hysterics and instead did this one thing. All the unseemly heaving and sweating would displace her for a moment into some oblivion of forgetting, but just as quickly, memories would flood her again, and she'd curl into a ball facing away from him as soon as the act was done.

All Mr. Thomas knew was that he was witness to a cache of emotion he hadn't known possible—the way she scratched and wept and pleaded for more. He sank deep into her vulnerability, licked her skin washed daily with lye soap.

He started seeking her out now, in the tired time between dusk and nightfall. He couldn't name exactly what it was that propelled him, only that since that first day in his study when he had seen this savage, ravaged thing, he felt compelled to uncover her. Be amidst that earthy muskiness, over and under a body that when supine looks as fragile and inviting as any woman's does. The revelation that she was in fact a woman. Strong, bronze. Her hair—coarse, thick. Real hair to tug. A lot suddenly seemed real to him. This woman who shook him, but would not look at him, awakened a passion he'd never experienced before.

In the evening he'd watch his wife Susan in front of the mirror, seeing the shadow of her nipples under the modest nightgown, her breasts rising as she reached up with her right arm to comb her auburn hair down her back, knowing she would soon be next to him, that hair spread out against the pillow, catching in his mouth as he turned during fitful sleep, and him feeling this strange sensation that she was just a body, just breath.

Things grow in time. Understanding, resentment. Evenings grew colder as the winter grew closer, light growing dim. The water, now dark in the night, radiated rings, Elizabeth stepping in up to her ankles. She unfurled Major's shirt, wrinkled from being bound too tight for so long, and laid it flat on the water. Watched the river carry the last traces of him away. She reached down and picked up a piece of jagged feldspar, briefly letting its edges graze the inside of her wrist before releasing it from her grip, placing her hands on her belly. She stared at the silent waves, wondering how something could grow in all this grief.

*   *   *

Finishing school didn't prepare Susan for the possibility that her husband might set his sights on the Negress maid. When she had first noticed Elizabeth's belly start growing, she didn't think much about it. She had the vague impression that colored people made love quite a lot so it did not surprise her, but beyond that, it seemed a subject not worth pondering. In fact, Susan found it a serendipitous opportunity to relieve the maid of her duties for a time. After several fine years—if she were honest, Elizabeth had quietly saved her when her own babies were born—the maid had inexplicably brought a certain malaise into the house, seemingly overnight. Stopped that way of singing they have—pleasant, oddly deep—and shuffled in heavy silence instead. Susan didn't like to feel uncomfortable in her own home.

Though the fact remained that she often was. She had learned her lessons well: how to charm dinner guests with witty tales that would not threaten their intelligence or cause any controversy, save a well-placed allusion to something more risqué. She had taken up quaint hobbies like knitting and gardening, though she felt enthusiasm for neither. She knew a few sonatas that she could play competently on the upright piano in the den; these same sonatas she would sometimes tap out over and over again when she felt at a loss for what to do during an empty hour. She had done a good job, landed a lawyer well on his way to becoming a judge. And that was it, wasn't it, for a long time. Fulfilled her cotillion calling. The days afterwards stretched long.

When she saw Elizabeth slip into Jefferson's study just after the new year, she was taken aback. She stood in the hallway for a long time, not knowing whether to follow her in or wait. Perhaps wait so long that Elizabeth wouldn't come back out and Susan would realize she had imagined it. She'd had the fortitude to imagine things, once upon a time.

Susan had only been in Jeff's study a few times over the years. It was one of those off-limits places that men have. When she herself had snuck in, she couldn't quite think what it was that went on in there. The air close with stale cigar smoke, the overflowing if ordered floor-to-ceiling bookshelves, various papers strewn about—it didn't seem all that appealing to her.

Susan wondered if perhaps Jeff had asked Elizabeth to clean his study along with the rest of the house. It certainly was in need of it. That he would have anything to do with the maid, though, was unlikely. These home matters were her (one and only) provenance. She stood in the passageway, feeling rather feeble. Direct confrontation was not the way of a Southern woman, with one's own kind at least, but with the help it certainly could be expected. She had never mastered that iron-gloved balance that her mother tried to impart to her. Oh, her fastidious mother. How she would have winced at the way Susan dawdled there so indecisively, gazing at the family portrait in the hall.

Susan must have rooted around too long in this—the familiar feeling of doubt, mixed with the complicated anger, love, and loss she felt whenever she contemplated her mother, so recently taken by that horrible coughing disease—because by the time she turned back and walked into the study, Elizabeth was already gone. Slipped out like she slipped in. Or had she at all? Susan felt unnerved, could not imagine the state of fluster she would be in if Jefferson were to now find *her* in here. She hurried out.

"How was work today?" she asked, sliding into bed later that night, having completed her ritual hair brushing. She always used the time to collect herself. When the twins had come—after all that time of trying, all that time of failing— the shock of sudden cries without warning spiraling down the corridor at unreasonable hours, she had special need for quiet moments. Even if they would shriek, each alarming the other, she would stay anchored in the chair until her hair rested sufficiently smooth.

Early on, too, she had realized the seductive overtones in her nightly routine, enjoyed catching Jeff looking at her, that trick of mirrors, like eyes in the back of your head. Lately he wasn't looking up from the bed as much, and when he did, there was almost a vacancy she couldn't place.

"Sammy, the same goddamned drunk," he was saying. "I almost feel like telling Jeb to stop giving him those tickets for disturbing the peace. Who the hell cares? He's more of a nuisance taking up time in a courtroom than he is out on the street. Do you know he started crying today? No shame."

Susan nodded. She had not wanted him to really engage the question, only mutter a *fine*, an *ok*, the kinds of monosyllables she was receiving recently, this house suddenly full of mutes: the sullen maid, the unresponsive husband. The twins, now toddlers, the most effusive, with their garbled nonsense. It was all becoming a bit insufferable.

Tonight a *harrumph* would have sufficed, however. She hated bothering Jeff with trifles, or bringing anything up that he might think was so. It amazed her how light-footed she could still feel around him.

"I think I saw Elizabeth enter your study today, Jeff."

He didn't respond, only glared harder at the book he held open on his lap. Susan shifted uncomfortably.

"I was thinking it might be time to let her go, anyway. She'll be having a baby soon. We, I mean, I can find someone else."

"What do you mean you *think* you saw her go into my study? Do you think or do you know?" he said, eyes still fixed on the page.

"Well, I…I guess she did. I just was surprised, I mean…"

"You guess. You think. You mean. Can you ever just be certain about something?" He fixed his gaze on her now. Unflinching.

"I'm sorry, Jeff, I thought you'd want to know," she said. Backpedaling. Made to stumble.

"Yes, I'd like to *know*. It doesn't sound like you know much of anything."

Susan fought back the sting in her eyes, didn't want to cry after he had just been complaining about poor emotional Sammy. Jeff's voice was one of the first things that had impressed Susan. She had easily pictured the handsome young boy before her presiding over a hearing with all heads turned up towards him, gavel in hand, baritone resonating in the chamber. That young boy who told her he attended Emory Law School, just like his father. That boy in Atlanta, the center of it all, for whom she'd wait on weekends when he'd return home to see her. To have that commanding voice turned so coldly towards her smarted.

"Well, she is pregnant. That is something I definitely know."

Jeff nodded. It seemed he had departed for some other place already. She hadn't believed the maid's family situation would be of much interest to him. What was this odd venom? It was neither interest nor disinterest, but something else. A meaning she was missing.

Susan turned out the light on her side of the bed and lay down, turning her head away from Jeff. She lay there for a few moments before she let the tears drop onto her pillow. Her crying came softly, but still audible. She pushed her face deeper into the pillow. At this, she felt Jeff move closer and wrap himself around her.

*   *   *

There aren't so much clues as a realization that there might be clues to find. One starts doubting the exterior of things. Faces suddenly seem absurd, the way they move this way and that, struggling to maintain neutral, often succeeding, when really, they're nothing but a mask. The banal stays the same—two sugars in lukewarm coffee, the way he lays the mail on the front table, always at an angle—but it all seems strangely foreign at the same time, like a puppet show, someone just pulling strings.

Things looked blank, like the slate sky that had moved in for the winter. Amazing how absence could suddenly replace what before had seemed present, full. Susan would stand on the porch staring at a gray sky that seemed infinite and one-dimensional at the same time. Flat. And extending forever.

It was not the best of seasons.

*   *   *

By autumn, the transgressions of nine months before had full shape. Though the August sun had left for September, a Southern fall still warm. The house fan whirred—Elizabeth hadn't heard her come into the kitchen. Susan watched as Elizabeth stooped down to pick up some bits of food—onion skins, chopped peppers—that had fallen during supper preparation. With her belly so big—god, any day now—the task looked arduous. Susan remembered her own time, when she was relegated to the bed for weeks. As if being pregnant were a sickness. As if holding a child made you weak.

Still, she felt awkward. Thought almost that she should help around the house—*god, her own goddamned house*—but it didn't seem quite proper, did it?

"Everything all right, Elizabeth?"

"Oh." Elizabeth stumbled to her feet. The *yes ma'ams* were slow in coming lately. The energy for pretense falling away with each passing day.

"You know, if you need to slow down, take a day off here or there, that's perfectly reasonable."

"Yes, ma'am. Thank you."

"It is hard to know how we'd manage without you, but we can probably get through on our own if need be." Susan smiled, a strained, wan smile. Her only job was pretense, but she was getting worse at her job, too.

Elizabeth turned around, easier to avoid Susan's eyes that way. The scraps still in her hand, she walked over to the sink and opened the cabinet below for the rubbish. She let out a moan, grabbed onto the counter. Another tiny yell, and she seemed to crumple.

"What is it Elizabeth?" Susan rushed over.

She gingerly took Elizabeth's hand in hers—warm, not as coarse as she had presumed. Almost soft, like hers. Was that a consolation? She had never touched black skin before, tried not to think of that black skin on him.

Susan led Elizabeth, who had to stop twice more as pains shot through her body, to the den.

"Now just sit here. I'll call the doctor," she said, leaving Elizabeth to make her way down to the sofa.

Susan walked into the hallway and dialed Doctor Andrews' number. She looked in the mirror as she listened to the low rings. These days, it took her a second to recognize her own reflection.

"Yes, Dr. Andrews. This is Susan Thomas. I'm well, thank you. It seems my maid, however, is in some need. She's with child, you see, and she's having some pains. No, no, not yet, just pain. Yes, thank you."

Susan walked back towards the den, her voice carrying down the hallway. "Dr. Andrews is on his way, don't worry. I told him it might be a false alarm, your…"

In the doorway, Susan stopped. Elizabeth was hunched over, her shoulders shaking, small sobs rising. It looked like she had cried herself a pool, the couch and rug below the mahogany table dripping wet. Elizabeth repeating, "I'm sorry, I'm sorry."

The sudden flood had always seemed the most distasteful to Susan. Something almost sordid. "That's what happens," she said, eyeing the maid's deluge, all over her furniture.

Both their heads turned at the sound of the door swinging shut.

"Let's see who that could be," Susan said, heading towards the front, happy for an excuse to leave the unseemly scene behind.

"Oh, dear," she said, watching Jeff place his hat on top of the coat rack.

"What's with the pale face?"

"Oh, well, just a bit of an adventure here."

"What? Doesn't adventure wait for me?"

Jefferson was heading towards his back study, when he passed by the opening to the den. Susan watched him stiffen, pause.

"Adventure?" he said. Elizabeth's legs splayed, liquid all around her. His whole body had tensed, his voice, too. "I should get her home."

"Dr. Andrews is on his way. It would be silly to move her now." Susan lowered her voice to a whisper. "She's in labor."

"One could see that," he snapped.

"Who knows what you men know."

"I'm going to take her home. She should be around her people."

"I really don't know…"

"I'm taking her home. It will be better."

"Well…"

"Susan, this is no place for this," he said harshly.

He walked into the den, unsure at first, then with more purpose. She watched him kneel down in his black suit, his right knee dipping into the liquid, his arms wrapping around Elizabeth, helping her up. Yes, this was no place for it. Shared fluids, entangled limbs. Here, people avoiding each other, everyone's breath held waiting to see the color of the coming child. The lightest shade of brown a colored child could be?

Jefferson had his right arm slipped around Elizabeth's waist, the two limping toward the front door together, him trying to hurry her along now, the panic starting to rise. Susan followed behind them, held the screen door open as she watched him pile Elizabeth into the car. He went around to the other side and started the ignition. He started backing up, then turned around—remembered. Gave a small wave before driving away.

What do men know? Susan wondered, as she watched the Buick disappear into the falling dusk. A woman knows when a man is lying. Can feel it in her bones. Notices the slack hand as he brushes you by accident, no longer by design. An extra inch distance between you lying in the marital bed. And you just have to take it, tell yourself not to measure the pressure of his hand or the space as you sleep. Just sit there as he pretends to read in the den and remind yourself that the faraway look in his eye once had to do with you.

TWO

(1977)

G reer stayed inside with Elizabeth as much as he could the first few days, sat by her bed, studied the face whose features found echo in his own—the same curve of jaw, their similar copper tone. Now Elizabeth's face wore pain, a different kind than he was used to seeing on her. He tried mentioning treatment again several times, but each time he was met with a stony silence. So what was he doing here? The Reverend's letter hadn't warned him that she wouldn't even admit to being sick.

The stale smell, the stiff silence, they reminded him too much of old times. When he couldn't stand it any longer, he'd go out for fresh air, stand on the porch and try to collect himself. How was he supposed to talk her into anything when they had never even found a way to talk back then?

Besides his mother's silence, much about Bannen had stayed the same. Esse still lived across the street; her child, Ceiley was often outside, too. Several times as he sat on the porch or went to Wilson's on errands, he noticed the girl glancing shyly his way. She had a slightly awkward way of walking and seemed always to carry a book. Greer felt a pang for her. Still just as hard to be different around here, he mused.

The Tuesday after his return, as he sat on the porch, he saw Ceiley carrying a small cage, a bird's song accompanying her. Due to no obstacle he saw, Ceiley tripped, both she and the cage tumbling to the ground. Greer sprang up and ran over to her. The cage was already broken, the bird flown away.

"Kid," he said, helping her up. "Is this mainly what you do for fun around here? Fall?"

Ceiley looked up at him and he saw tears brimming in her eyes, though he saw defiance there, too. This wasn't the time to tease her.

"Hey, it's ok," he said. "No one's hurt."

"The bird," she said. "It's gone."

"Yeah. But maybe it's better that way."

"Why?" she said. "I wanted that bird. Have something of my own."

"Some things aren't for owning," Greer said. "How would you like to be put in a cage?"

Ceiley looked down at the broken enclosure and mumbled something.

"What?" Greer said.

"Yeah," she muttered.

"I just mean, maybe the bird should be free." Greer bent down and picked up the birdcage. Its door hung open at an odd angle, only one hinge still in place. "Like, hey," he said, "do you ever feel stuck here in Bannen?"

"Yeah!" Ceiley said, lighting up.

"Thought so. Not a good feeling, right?"

"No," she said shaking her head, but growing visibly excited.

"And imagine, we have the air to breathe, we can walk where we please. There's nothing really holding us back."

"Yeah, except everything."

Greer nodded. He knew about everything.

"Well, just think about it. No bars," he said opening his arms wide.

Ceiley beamed at him, stood there like she was waiting for something else.

"Well, watch your step, ok?" he said.

He turned around to go, but not to the house. He didn't want to go back there yet; he needed light. He started walking down the street, his thoughts keeping pace. Thoughts that were always with him, in some form or another. The ties that bind, the invisible cages that contain you wherever you go.

Greer could feel Ceiley's eyes still on him, though. He wasn't so lost in thought that he didn't feel her gaze burning the back of his shirt.

Greer stopped. Sighed. Put his thumb and forefinger to the bridge of his nose. Finally he turned around.

"You want to go bird-watching, kid?" he yelled out to her. "Out in the wild?"

Ceiley came bounding towards him. The loose door of the cage banged against the bars as she ran, then continued as she walked beside him. Neither of them let on that they noticed.

THE GIFT

(1958)

Another woman has lost her man. That was what Elizabeth thought as she watched Mrs. Phillips carry her husband's things out onto the lawn—one shirt or boot or work glove at a time—and set fire to each article until it left nothing but ash in the same small area on the grass. Whether it was the smoke or her crying that kept a constant glisten of tears on Mrs. Phillips' face was hard to tell.

Elizabeth sat on the porch, breathing in the fumes that had risen to blanket the entire block. There was nothing to be done to combat the smell, or the heat from the flames, but this did not bother her. A fire eventually burned itself out; smoke eventually cleared. Fire's opposite, however, was another matter.

Several people had passed by the last few days to offer support to Mrs. Phillips, but she only railed at them to let her be, there wasn't any crime in getting rid of things no one could ever use again. "Do you want a dead man's shoes?" Elizabeth heard her scream.

The steady trickle of people had stopped for the day, either because it was suppertime or they couldn't stand the smoke in their eyes. For Elizabeth, the fluid that gathered in hers was actually a comfort. It was simply a physical reaction to the chemicals in the air; for once the tears were not sourced from anything personal—at least not personal for her.

Mrs. Phillips fell to the ground where she lay among the smoking embers of her husband's things. Her daughter Esse— still a little girl whose cornrows were starting to unravel—came to stand near her mother, but Mrs. Phillips swiped her hand out at her and said something harsh to make the girl run back into the house.

Elizabeth judged. At least she resolved to never raise her voice or hand to her child, she thought, no matter how strong grief tugged at her. Her form of grief, in fact, was to keep as quiet and still as she could, as if keeping herself small was a way to get as close to Major's condition as possible; an apology that she was still alive and he wasn't.

Elizabeth saw Reverend Smith walking up Main Street and was surprised when he turned towards her house rather than Mrs. Phillips' once he neared. She did not greet him until she was sure it was her he had come to see. A slight sweat had already broken out over his brow, but whether it was the heat of the continuing fire or his discomfort as he glanced at Mrs. Phillips' public display was uncertain. He had already stopped by several times to offer his condolences, but each time his words fell short of her towering pain.

"Evening to you, Miss Elizabeth. How are you holding up?"

"Better than our sister across the way." Elizabeth did not feel particularly close to Mrs. Phillips—certainly not like a sister—but she always took on a certain kind of language with the Reverend. She was still uneasy in his presence; she had never completely forgiven him.

"Yes, that's what I've come to talk to you about in fact," he said, taking his hat off as he reached the top step of the porch.

"Oh?" Elizabeth said.

"Sing for the service," he said, coming right to the point.

"I think it would help our sister heal to have you send Robert off that way. You know how much he loved good gospel."

This was the last thing Elizabeth expected and it made her throat tighten. She didn't say anything, but he stood there waiting expectantly and she knew he would not move until she answered him. "You know I don't sing anymore, Reverend," she said finally.

"Yes, and that was another great loss to the community," he said. "Bannen hasn't been the same since you gave it up."

Elizabeth didn't say anything for a moment. Then, "I'm not that important, Reverend."

He gave her an intense look as if to contradict, then faced Mrs. Phillips' fire again.

"Things have been heating up around here," he said. "We need a little inspiration."

Elizabeth bowed her head. It *had* been gruesome of late. Robert Phillips caught in that machine at the mill. Poor Ed Starling before that, and his friends who'd had to cut him down from the tree. Fear was starting to grip East Bannen.

Elizabeth turned her gaze back to Mrs. Phillips, who had been cursing and pleading and blaming and crying on and off for 72 hours now, and she wondered if her own voice still had the power to match that of this bereaved woman's. She wanted the Reverend to step down off her porch, to take the question away, to realize how wrong it was for him to ask something of her that she so clearly had erased for herself, had thought she had erased for everybody after all these years.

Still, he was right, too. Things felt different, people more scared. But could she really do anything to help?

"I'll think on it," she said.

"Pray on it, Sister. Pray on it. It's another's time of need.

Don't be selfish with your gift," he said, before taking his leave.

She watched him walk across the street and lay his hand on Mrs. Phillips' shoulder, only to have her violently shrug it off.

Elizabeth did nothing like praying as she tossed the idea around in her mind, but she did think. She did remember. Suddenly the smoke burned her eyes and she couldn't stand hearing the woman weep anymore. She went into the house and closed the door on the sight, though the sound still echoed within her.

*   *   *

On the day of the service, Wilson's General was only open in the early morning for folks who hadn't had time to fix something to bring to the wake. After that, all of East Bannen crowded into the church to hear what new way the Reverend would try to frame something as old and common as death. In these recent cases, something as cold and senseless, too.

Elizabeth did not sing in the church, however, but rather as Robert Phillips' casket was lowered into the ground. She was glad it turned out that way, as she couldn't imagine singing in that church she had left so many years before. She sat and listened to the sermon unmoved. There was no way to explain why life was so suddenly yanked from someone, and any attempt only seemed contrived and false. The Reverend had tried to explain things to her after Major was taken. Had, in fact, told her this was an opportunity to submit herself more fully to the grace of God. How he could have said that, talked of God's mysterious ways, was enough to make her retch. How he had then slid his hand on her in a way that seemed a touch too familiar to emphasize his point only made it worse. It had gone no further, his form of comfort, but it was enough for her to cease believing altogether in grace of any kind.

The soil being thrown on Robert Phillips' casket had stones in it, and they made a thumping noise as they landed on the wood. A shovelful, then another, and on one such thump, Elizabeth suddenly saw an image she hadn't thought of since it happened: her bloody footprints on the linoleum floor. On that dark night long ago, she hadn't noticed the sharp rocks cutting her feet until she saw the blood she tracked inside.

Dust now rose from the ground, as the open hole in the earth gradually filled with dirt. The dust made the air hazy, and even out there in the bright sun she thought of the dark night and the fog that had made it hard to see. Everything was coming back now; her senses were full.

When she opened her mouth it was like all the sorrow she had tried to contain spilled forth in a deluge. Sound hemorrhaging, as if her body were rejecting something which was not good for it: the sadness, the unspoken, the many years of regret. The voice seemed almost outside of herself, like it had a life of its own.

Elizabeth closed her eyes. She was no longer at Robert Phillips' funeral, she had not been bidden by the Reverend to soothe another woman's pain. How could she when she had so much of her own? She wasn't there for Esse, either, yet another child now deprived a father. Elizabeth sang and she thought not of the fire she had watched the whole week, but rather of water, its seeming innocence, a gentle lapping that turned fatal and drowned those caught in it. At Robert Phillips' funeral, Elizabeth was singing for a dead man, but it was not the man being buried, but Clayton Major, *her* Major, that sweet man she had lured into the water with her voice and had lost forever. The dust and the stones, and the cold water of Sicama River that had killed him. The source of life, the source of death; she sang it all to the depths.

*   *   *

There were still people in town who remembered that Miss Elizabeth had the most beautiful voice of anyone in Bannen, and when they heard her sing, after more than a dozen years without it, they wondered how they could ever have let it slip from their minds, even if just for a second. A voice like that sets you to remembering.

When she opened her mouth and made her music, majestic, it seemed hard to believe it was only one woman and not the full choir producing such a rich sound. People stood mesmerized; they didn't know whether to cry at the truths she gave voice to or feel joy that such beauty could exist on earth, that such a gift as hers could be made manifest.

In that crowd, the person most moved by Miss Elizabeth's voice, however, was her only son Greer, whose own voice had recently become untrustworthy. He could never be sure now if he could hold it steady, or if it would rise or fall several registers without warning. Greer, who had never known his mother could sing at all, who, if truth be told, hardly ever knew more than a weak, small voice to come out of her, watched his mother open her mouth wide and emit a sound that seemed to emanate from somewhere deeper than he knew possible, her eyes closed, choosing to see something inside rather than look out at the crowd. Choosing not to look at him.

Greer started shaking; it could have been her voice—it was powerful enough to shake the ground—but it was also something inside him breaking and something forming in its place. How could his mother have hidden this for all these years? It was as if he could hear what the vast silence he lived with could have been filled with. Elizabeth had never sung him so much as a lullaby.

Greer looked up and saw a bird fly across the sky, its swooping arc almost mirroring the rise and fall of the notes Elizabeth's clear timbre gave shape to. He looked back down at his mother and she looked different than he'd ever seen her before. She looked rounder, more full. She even looked wise for a moment, like someone who had things to say. He knew nothing about the people who had made him. No wonder he didn't know who he was.

* * *

The end of Elizabeth's song came too quickly, the air suddenly denied the sound that had so completely filled it just a moment before. She blinked her eyes rapidly a few times; she seemed unable to focus on any one face in the crowd. Her gaze finally found her son, but she didn't recognize the stiffness he was carrying as anything more than an old suit too tight in the shoulders.

There were some audible sounds of grief now, as if the crowd had been too stunned before to start in on their wailing. Their crying swelled like a wave. At its crest, Elizabeth bowed her head then turned away. She started walking slowly towards home. After a moment, Greer followed her.

THREE

(1977)

"Is there anything I can do, Mama?" Greer asked Elizabeth.

"No, baby, you're here. That's more than enough."

Greer sat by the side of the bed, wondered how this could be enough for her. How any of this could have ever been enough.

"Doctor says you have to go for treatment. Just resting won't cure anything."

"Don't know why you called him over. No point in going in for magic cures."

"You have to do something. It's only going to get worse if you stay here like this."

"A person's time comes when it does."

"God, why didn't you just give up years ago then?" Greer said, getting up, the chair nearly falling over with his force.

Elizabeth's face scrunched up in pain. "I had you, baby."

"Uh-huh, a lot of good it did me," he said.

"What are you talking about now, baby? What are—"

Greer cut her off. "So it's just like it always was, right?

We're just going to pretend like I haven't been gone, like you're not dying, like there's nothing real to talk about."

"You never used to be angry like this," Elizabeth said, struggling to sit up in bed.

"I didn't know what there was to be angry about."

"Baby…" What words did she have? None.

"You never told me." Greer paced the room. "Did you ever give that letter to Caroline? Do you know what happened to her?" he asked abruptly.

Elizabeth didn't say anything. She just squinted her eyes.

"I know you know who I'm talking about. Well did you?"

Elizabeth shook her head.

"No, you didn't give it to her? Or no, you don't know what happened?" Greer stopped pacing and looked right at his mother. "Or no to everything, just like always?"

Elizabeth's eyes had grown big. Seemed she could do nothing but shake her head.

"No, I…" she began and then stopped. She clutched her hand against her heart as a pain shot through her.

"Are you ok?" Greer asked.

"I don't know," Elizabeth said.

Greer leaned over. "Where does it hurt? I'm sorry, Mama."

"I don't know," she said again. "I heard Caroline moved away."

Greer straightened up, then shook his head. "I don't know where she is, either," he said. "I tried to find out. Couldn't do anything from over there."

Elizabeth put her hand on his back. So seldom had she reached out to him.

Greer placed a hand over his face and let it slide down. "None of this was supposed to happen like this," he said.

"No," she agreed.

"None of it."

*   *   *

Greer brought home new washers from Wilson's and gleaming silver pipes. Wrenches, screwdrivers—just about every tool known to man. In the kitchen, he opened the doors underneath the sink and slowly unscrewed the plumbing, laying each piece on the floor. He peered inside the clogged pipes, saw what must be decades' worth of buildup. He rubbed his hands against his khaki pants. Streaks of rust appeared.

After fitting the pipes and changing the washers, he tested the water's flow; it stopped on cue when he turned off the tap.

Such a simple task: replacing the old parts with new, taking everything apart and putting it back together. Greer had not come back for this, but he realized just the same: he'd have to disassemble everything if he were to move forward. What he would put back in its place, though, he really couldn't say.

*   *   *

That night, as with every night since his return, Greer sat on the back steps until it grew dark, not bothering to turn on the lights. The porch out front was fine for day, but by the time dusk fell, he didn't want to risk seeing anyone pass by. Small talk was impossible.

"Can't see anything out there like that, can you?" Elizabeth would ask before going off to bed.

It didn't matter if he could see. He could feel the heavy air press on him, the humidity as oppressive as Ghana during the wet season.

Ghana. Gloria. Had it only been a couple weeks since he'd been there with her? A good woman who'd almost made him whole again. He had even started thinking about a future, as much as the past. She had sent him back with her blessing. Yet here he was in Bannen, thinking constantly of Caroline. Consumed again.

He had been afraid this was going to happen. But how could he have told Gloria that? He was supposed to be here for his mother.

Greer swatted at a mosquito that landed on his upper left arm, but another quickly took its place. Frustrated by all that swarmed in his head, around him, he stood up and went back inside the house with no light.

THE BURN

(1961)

Even in darkness the white Thunderbird gleamed, its curved lines caressing the night. Called a bullet for the body's shape, the name might as well have described their meetings way out here: Loaded. Dangerous. Fast.

Caroline parked the car deep in the woods, the engine still humming as she switched off the ignition, then stepped outside. When she shut the door, the sound seemed to rattle all the branches, disturb the birds in their nests. Whole flocks flew, the star-shaped leaves of sweetgum trees swayed above their heads as they leaned against the humming metal.

It was one of those impossible summers—sweltering, sultry. Like every summer, like every night. Even with the vinyl top down, the car breathed heat. Steam bathed everything, a world glistening with sweat.

"Look what I did," she said, turning to face the car, lifting up her dress a little to show him the back of her thighs.

Greer bent down cautiously, reached out a tentative hand. "Does it hurt?" he said, tracing a finger along her skin, which even in the dark he could see was red.

"It burns," she said.

"You have to be careful, take your time," he said, his own heat rising, squatting behind her like that. "Those seats will burn you if you don't let them cool off first."

"I couldn't wait. I just wanted to get to you."

And Greer wanted her. He dropped to his knees, his face now just an inch away from her secret place. Before he even knew what he was doing, he leaned forward and ran his tongue over the burn, kissed her thigh. She tasted salty and sweet. Caroline gave a short gasp of surprise.

"Does that make it better?" he asked.

"Yes," she said, short of breath.

Greer didn't know what to do now; Caroline seemed to sense his hesitation.

"Go on," she said, though towards what, neither of them were sure. They had never done this part before. "Dare."

Greer slid his hands up her thighs. Caroline leaned forward across the long hood. He slipped her underwear off, then made his way back up her legs with his mouth, but continued climbing this time. When he reached the top, he put his mouth there, too. Even saltier, even more juice.

After, they both lay on the hood, clasping hands, so tender, so tight.

"The whole world feels different with you," he said. "Everything's new."

"I know," she said. "It's like we've just been born."

FOUR

(1977)

Ceiley shuffled down Main Street. She couldn't stop looking at her feet. Yes, they were still growing, that was for sure. Seemed like she was getting too big for everything—her shoes, her room, this town. Too big for her britches her mama would say. Size 10 sneakers were in order, in any case, and none too soon. The white Keds she had been trying to keep clean had lost the fight to Bannen's soil long ago. A new shade of brown had appeared, or maybe she was just now noticing. Had she dropped molasses on them this morning? Ceiley leaned over to take a closer look at the new smudge on her shoes, misjudging her ability to do so easily. She tripped, and it was only on the way down that she heard the distinctive sound of tires on dry dirt.

"You again," Greer said over the screeching. "What did I tell you about looking up?"

Ceiley regained her footing, leaning heavy on her left leg. Her arms hung long at her sides. She felt like a gorilla.

"You get in trouble with your mother the other day?" he said, gracefully moving past the subject of her gracelessness.

Ceiley could see what he meant. First she was storming out of the house when they met, then she just took off with him to go birdwatching without telling Esse where she was going.

"It's ok. I'm always in trouble," she muttered.

"You are, are you? What does a troublemaker do around here for fun?"

"Oh, I don't know. I'm not really. Just, you know, my mama's always on me for something."

"Aw, I'm sure she's just looking out for you. Your mama's supposed to do that—treat you like you're special. Bet you are."

That was a new one, at least how it felt coming from him. Ceiley had wanted to feel anything but special lately. Standing out was no gift.

"Where are you off to?" he asked.

"Wilson's, get some fruit."

"Yeah, what's your favorite?" he asked.

Ceiley snorted. "There's not much choice around here is there?" *Apple with one p, chicken scrawl on the store's sign, this town so small it's stupid...*

Greer was pedaling and backpedaling, trying to go slow enough on the bike to ride alongside her. His handlebars swung from side to side.

"Same old apples and oranges, eh?"

"Yeah," Ceiley said.

Suddenly Greer's face lit up. "Hey, wait here a minute. I'll be back." He sped off and Ceiley looked around, to see if anyone was watching. She didn't want anyone to notice, but she was prepared to stand right there till he got back. Well, twiddling thumbs was nothing new in Bannen.

Five minutes later Greer came riding up, only his left hand on the handlebars, his right behind his back.

"Close your eyes," he said.

"What?"

"Just do it," he said, "and hold out your hands."

Ceiley did after a brief pause. She turned her head to one side and sighed, attempting to look bored, but she was anything but. What new excitement was this? She felt a weight placed in her hands. Her fingers cupped something cool and smooth.

"Bite," Greer said.

Ceiley opened her eyes, then narrowed them. She held half of some sort of odd fruit, the inside of it orange-gold, bright as the sun.

"Come on, I smuggled this in through customs," he said.

"What's customs?"

"Oh, you know, territorial bullshit." Ceiley didn't understand what Greer was talking about, but she liked the way he said it. Confident, conspiratorial.

"As long as it's something you eat," she said.

He grinned and nodded.

She took the fruit's flesh into her mouth. Sweet. Juicy. Unlike anything she'd tasted before. Soon, there was a mess. Strings caught in her teeth. Her hands grew sticky.

"You could have warned me," she said.

"Ha, but that's the best," he said. "Discovering for yourself."

Ceiley swallowed with a little difficulty. "So, what is this?" she said, switching the weight to her right leg.

"Mango," he said. Ceiley drew the word in her head. She liked the sound of it. "Do you know mango trees line every dirt road in Ghana?" Greer continued. "You'd think nothing could grow in ground like that, but then they do. Kid, like I say, you always got to look up."

He pressed his index finger to her chest then pushed her chin up when she looked down. She'd mind if other people did that, but with Greer, she didn't seem to. No, she liked it.

"Maybe we should have a talk with Wilson about adding some variety to his selection. What do you think?" Greer asked.

"Yeah, right. That old man? Like anything will ever change around here."

"Hey, there are some things you do have control over." Greer stopped pedaling. "Sometimes, you just have to try."

*   *   *

There was something magic about Greer. The simple fact that he was the only person Ceiley knew who had actually stepped foot outside of Bannen would have been enough, but then there was the assurance with which he rode these streets that just days before had seemed so impossibly dull. As if stepping off the edge of the world then coming back was the most natural thing to do. That's near to how her mother had described it, too. Said that Greer had just upped and left one day.

Her mother didn't seem to care one way or the other about the man, but made her little clucking noises that always accompanied any slight disapproval. Ceiley could guess why— he certainly didn't seem to have any religion. She felt something like jealousy that her mother had grown up across the street from him. Could have seen him a million times, sitting on the porch, walking by, swinging his lean arms to and fro. Though she acted like an old maid, her mother hadn't even reached thirty yet.

Ceiley pushed, but Esse had little to say about Greer. "Didn't never do no one harm," was the best she could offer.

The jealousy turned to the increasingly familiar rage; her mother's stupidity was not to be borne much longer, though she was relieved to hear her mother had no interest in the exotic stranger. Just more proof Esse was blind as a bat—couldn't see anything for what it really was.

Ceiley, on the other hand, looked out for him every chance she got now—would keep vigil by the window watching until she saw him leave his house, then scurry out herself, like she just happened to be leaving, too. By the wildest of surprises, he always seemed happy enough to see her, let her tag along.

"Kept to himself when I known him," Esse said. "Always had his nose in a book. No more sense than you," she added, in a harrumph.

As if she weren't already, that was enough for Ceiley to fall hopelessly in love with him.

INVISIBLE LIGHT

(1961)

When Greer was growing up, it sometimes seemed to him that Bannen was a town made only of women. They got groceries, hung the laundry out to dry, braided children's hair while sitting on worn front steps.

The men, they worked in the factory or tilled a soil too often stubborn on the outskirts of town. Migrants came and went. Men left early, returned home late. The ones he did see occupied small hours—the break of dawn or well after dusk, the time when the light plays tricks on the eyes. And even then, what could you really know? They moved quietly in the morning, but grew loud at night, liquid courage fueling deep voices. Only on Sundays did he see men alive for a full day, present from daylight to evening's end.

The comings and goings of men, returning in dirty overalls, sweat on their brows—Greer watched it all, looking for clues in their carriage. There was little he could glean. For a while it didn't seem so strange to him to think of his father as a ghost, what with this general absence.

His mother never talked about Major; it was a miracle Greer even knew his father's name or that he'd drowned before Greer was born. It almost made sense at first, this mythology. That's all he could call it afterwards.

Only a truth did hide in the myth, it was not lost in water: Man is elemental. You cannot hold water, but it is necessary for life. Greer had this great need to know his father, yet there was nothing of him. Greer, beating heart, blood, flesh and bone. How did he exist with half of himself unknown?

*   *   *

Greer stood on the edge of the river, trying to read the past in its black waves. With the night so dark and a quarter moon barely seeping light through the trees, all he could catch were glimpses of the hills and valleys of the water as it flowed along its way. He had taken to walking farther and farther along the banks of Snake Creek. With neither the river's beginning nor end in sight, it was both comforting and frightening to think of something extending forever.

Tonight he stopped at a spot where the river appeared to grow in both width and speed. Why did it suddenly change here? The river turned almost dangerous. For reasons he couldn't name, he felt compelled to jump in. He stripped off his clothes and let them drop in a heap.

The water was cooler than he expected. He felt the swift current immediately, its insistent tug testing his strength. The water beat against his back, his body battling the waves. What would happen if he just let go? He imagined giving in to the pull of the water, thought about this invisible force powerful enough to fell a man.

He swam back toward the bank, a place where he could stand in the water again. He closed his eyes and listened to the night. Like the dark river, his thoughts and feelings seemed limitless. He thought about spirits in the tide. Was his father still here, somewhere within these waves? Had he been strong like the current? Or had life already beat him down? What had his hands looked like, what could he hold? What would he have told Greer, if he were still here to speak to him?

Greer could have stayed there forever, carried away by questions, but he heard something foreign break the night. He opened his eyes and saw what seemed a small, sensuous form floating on land. Had his imaginings been that powerful? Did the spirit awake? He was ready, not scared; he'd been waiting a long time for this.

It was only when he realized the light was no ghost, but a white girl, that fear grabbed hold.

*   *   *

Greer watched the girl move toward the river. She seemed almost in a trance as she approached. His eyes veered from side to side. Could she see him? Was she alone? Could he swim away undetected?

Greer couldn't know it was the gush of the water, so generous and uninhibited, that drew Caroline, not anything in view. He couldn't imagine that just hours before she'd suffered a tight tulle gown and her coming out ball. To her, once again, an occasion of suffocation and the unceasing desire for escape.

So when she lifted her dress, it was her freedom—but his fear. Her clothes fell to the ground and Greer emitted an involuntary sound. Then, quickly, he ducked under the water. He held and held and held his breath, his pulse, his panic vibrating in the waves.

When he finally had to reach for air, he emerged to see her completely naked now, hugging the edge. She jumped, created a big splash, then, just as fast, got knocked down and tossed around, the swift current taking her off guard. Her voice was as surprised as scared, but there was no mistaking, soon after, her call for aid. We cry out even when we think we're alone.

For a split second, Greer froze, unable to calculate which was riskier—approaching the white girl and trying to help, or doing nothing and something happening to her, him being blamed.

There was no time to reflect, though; she was rapidly being carried farther and farther downstream. Impulse took over and he catapulted through the water, adrenaline coursing through his veins. His strokes were fast—they had to be.

He cut through the water, swam as hard as he could. When he reached her, he had no choice but to touch, wrap his arms around her lithe frame. With his right arm gripped tightly around her waist, he swam them both to the eastern shore. He grunted as he struggled to lift her up, then collapsed, right on top of her.

Greer was completely winded, Caroline sputtering water. For several minutes the only sound was their ragged breathing as they sought large helpings of air.

"So strong," Caroline finally said. "The current."

Greer managed only a word: "Dangerous."

Caroline, short of breath, looked him straight in the eye, full of wonder. "You saved my life. You know what that means?"

Greer, still stunned, shook his head.

"Now we're bound forever."

Greer realized he was still holding her, still on top of her. So close, too close, naked chests rising and falling. Could she feel his heart pounding?

He tried to remember himself. "I'm sorry, Miss," he

said, and began to move away. Her watery beauty was almost frightening, but it was the way she looked at him so boldly that made him tremble.

"Don't worry," she said, seeming to hold him in place. "I'm harmless."

Harmless didn't seem the word; the electricity between them threatened to shock. Greer felt his fear rising, along with something else. He rolled away quickly this time and reached out for his clothes lying nearby. He dressed as fast as he could, trying to hide his erection.

He could sense her sitting up after a moment, hear her slowly stand up. He willed himself not to turn around. *Don't dare.*

Caroline came around to face him, her dress now clinging to her, her hair, mouth, wet.

"I'm cold now," she said, running her hands up and down her arms.

He nodded. It was all he could offer.

She shivered, wrapped her arms tight around herself. "How do I thank you?"

"You don't have to thank me, Miss."

"Yes I do. I'm so stupid to have jumped in like that."

Greer neither denied nor confirmed this.

"But what were you doing out there?" she asked.

He could barely think, could barely remember anything before she came along. What was *she* doing out here? But he knew well enough—you only answer their questions.

"I don't know, Miss. Thinking."

"Oh, stop calling me Miss," she flicked her hand. "I think we're past formalities after all that, don't you?"

"I don't know, Miss. Sorry."

She looked out at the water, then back at Greer. After a long pause she asked, "You always go in the water to think?"

"Just looking for something," he said, surprising himself.

"Oh yeah? Like mermaids?" Caroline gave a short laugh. "Damsels in distress?"

Greer shook his head. "I don't know."

"What *do* you know?"

Greer shrugged helplessly. He knew that the goosebumps on his arm had nothing to do with the night breeze against wet skin and everything to do with this mysterious white girl before him. He knew he should be finding the fastest way out of there, but he stood fast, entranced.

"I don't know much either," Caroline said, crossing her arms again and turning to the water. She stared out for a few moments. "But I know that was magic," she said, turning back to him. "Out of nowhere, you swooping in like my guardian angel or something."

Greer didn't say anything.

"I want magic, you know?" she said.

He didn't respond.

"Don't you?"

Greer stayed silent for a minute, then nodded so slight she'd have missed it if she weren't staring at him so hard. She reached out and touched his arm. He started at her touch.

"Hey," she said, withdrawing her hand. "You really are nervous. I thought you were bold, the way you came and got me, but really you're shy."

"Don't know what to say, Miss."

"Let's forget every stupid rule we were ever taught, ok? It's just little old me."

"And…you are?" he asked, finally allowing himself a question.

"Nobody," she said, shaking her head.

Greer tightened his lips. Nodded.

"What?" she said.

"I'm nobody, too."

Caroline brightened. "'Then there's a pair of us—don't tell!'"

"I won't tell," Greer said, thinking he sure couldn't tell anyone about this. But that line—it couldn't help but strike him. "Emily Dickinson?" he asked tentatively.

Caroline's eyes widened. "Yeah," she said. "You know it, too?"

He nodded.

"'How dreary to be somebody!'" she quoted.

"'How public, like a frog.'"

"'To tell your name the livelong day.'"

Greer looked at her with even more wonder. Who was this girl?

"I don't know anyone else who memorizes poetry," she said.

"Me neither."

They stood looking at each other, not knowing what to say now. Caroline started running her hands up and down her arms again. He couldn't stand to see her shaking like that, though he was still shaking himself, too.

"I wish I could give you something to keep warm."

Caroline stopped moving, just looked at him. "It's amazing," she said. "You shimmer. Glow."

Greer felt his cheeks grow hot. He had always hoped before then that his skin found cover under darkness, his difference hidden by the night.

"I wish I were invisible sometimes," he whispered.

"Yeah?" she said. "You can do a lot when you're invisible." They looked at each other, then Caroline reached out her hand. Greer, after a long pause, took it. They shook hands slowly.

"Two nobodies then. We won't tell."

*　　　*　　　*

In daylight, it didn't seem possible. How could it have been real? His damp clothes, a cold that had settled into his bones despite the heat, a scrape on his arm from bringing Caroline safely to the bank, these were all reminders that the whole night had happened. Still, it seemed like a dream.

Greer had something else, though, something to hold. Her necklace, which she had placed in his hand. "Carry me with you. Until we meet again."

There'd been no use saying it, they both knew: they were not to be seen. But it was clear they had seen each other—and they must come again.

Now in the stark sun, it seemed not smart in the least. Was he crazy? Colored boys who went near white girls— that always had a terrible end.

But for three days straight he'd been replaying every second of their encounter. As risky as it was, how could he *not* go to her tonight as they'd planned? Hadn't he always wanted to feel this alive?

"I want magic. Don't you?"

Greer ran his finger over the back of the locket, felt the ridges of the inscription: *Caroline* engraved in a thin cursive. He wanted to whisper the name over and over again. He realized he hadn't even told her his.

Greer waited impatiently for dusk. He decided he'd just have to be as careful as he could. All sorts of awful scenarios had played in his mind. Only, for some reason, he didn't believe any of them. A set-up? A trap? These were the things he was supposed to think.

But that space far out in the forest seemed like some magical place now, no East or West Bannen. All he knew was that Caroline had said he shimmered—and he thought she shined.

*   *   *

He had never been so aware of the sound of his footsteps before. His long solitary walks had always calmed him, but now his heart raced. He had rarely ever run into someone out this far, yet tonight he kept looking over his shoulder. Trying to see behind the trees.

When he arrived, she was already there. She sat on the edge of the water, her feet dangling in. Her hair hung loose down her back. He couldn't help thinking maybe she really was a mermaid—she seemed that strange and lovely.

He stayed a good few feet away and scanned the surroundings. Finally, he spoke up.

"Caroline?" he said, testing the name from the locket.

She turned. "I didn't know if you'd come."

He gave one last look around.

"What are you looking for?" she asked.

"Nothing."

Caroline took her feet from the water, hugged her legs to herself. "Hey, I know, ok? Don't worry about stuff like that."

Greer sat down across from her, but still kept a healthy distance.

"The world back there, it has nothing to do with us," she said.

"It wouldn't have us here together at all," he said.

"Well, you know what? I think the world is just stupid sometimes. Doesn't it just make you want to scream and get out of here?" Caroline pulled a pack of cigarettes out of her bag. "Plus, we're just two nobodies anyway, right? Why should anyone care?" She offered a cigarette to him. "Here, maybe these will relax you a little."

"I've never had one before," Greer said, taking it.

"Neither have I," she said and laughed.

"Really?" he said, allowing himself a small smile. "Why are you carrying these around then?"

"I lifted them today."

Greer nodded. There was nothing about this girl he understood. And yet everything she did intrigued him.

"God, I'm kidding," she said. "You think I'm slick enough to do something like that?"

"I think you could probably do anything you wanted."

"Well, that'd be nice to think so," she said, pulling a lighter from her purse. He could tell by the way she worked it that she really didn't know what she was doing. She couldn't get the lighter to catch.

"Want me to try?" he asked.

She extended the lighter out to him. They brushed hands and he felt the same shock as the first night.

"You must be made of sparks," she said.

Greer pressed the lighter; it took on his first try. He held the flame out to her. She leaned forward, the long filtered cigarette between her lips. She took a drag and immediately coughed.

"God," she said, "this is awful." She glanced at him, as he lit his own cigarette. He gave a short cough, too, but he managed better than her. Now she seemed like the nervous one. "I always seem to be out of breath when I'm around you."

He knew the feeling. He took another drag on his cigarette. Something about the action, having something to do, did relax him. He could barely breathe around this girl. Could barely swallow. The fire in his throat seemed appropriate.

"Hey, you caught on quick," she said.

Caroline tried a few more drags and kept coughing. "They don't show this part in the pictures." They smiled and fell silent for a few moments. It felt both natural and unnatural at the same time.

"I don't even know your name," she said after a while. "Why do I feel like I know you somehow?"

"Greer," he said. "Greer Michaels."

"Shh," she said. "No family names. We're not our parents' children. We have to make our own rules, right?"

Greer had to think about it. "I guess you could say that," he said. They wouldn't be out here otherwise. "Feels like I don't know anything about my parents." He looked out at the water, took a long drag on his cigarette. He smoked like he was born to it. "My father drowned in that river. Mama never talks about him."

"That's terrible. I'm sorry." Caroline was quiet for a moment. Then, "Is that why you were out there the other night? You feel closer to him swimming in the water or something?"

"I don't know," Greer said. "Maybe."

Caroline stared at the water, too. Her shoulders seemed to slump a little now. "It's strange how you can miss someone you never even knew." She tucked a strand of hair behind her ear. "I know what it's like."

Greer looked at her face—smooth, yet strong, like the bones underneath her pale skin were pushing their way out for attention. High and striking.

"You ever just feel left behind or something? Like people can be all around and you still feel alone?"

"All the time," Greer said.

Caroline nodded and they both fell back into silence. This remarkable girl was from some other planet as far as all he'd been taught, yet she voiced things he thought only he felt.

"So who are you looking for?" he asked.

Caroline flicked her free hand as if to wave away her seriousness. "Oh, never mind," she said. "I'm not much fun today, am I? Anyway, looks like I found you." She tried her cigarette again, which by this point had gathered a long line of ash. Her lungs were just as bothered as they were in the beginning. She laid her hand on her chest as she coughed again, then stubbed out her cigarette in the grass. "This really does taste terrible."

Greer wanted to know more about who it was that she missed. It was crazy. He didn't know anything about her and yet already he wanted to mean something to her, too. All thoughts soon left his mind, though, as Caroline inched a little closer, pretended like she hadn't.

Greer swallowed hard, looked around again. Caroline pulled at the grass, broke the blades, then threw them on the ground. Suddenly she clapped her hand over her mouth and laughed.

Greer half-smiled, not understanding.

"It's funny. They always smoke *after* in the movies."

Greer felt the fire from his throat start to move throughout his whole body.

When he didn't respond, she looked at him sheepishly. "Don't you think that's funny?"

Images were flooding his mind, but he wouldn't let his words betray him. Yes, he did have a funny feeling, but not in the way she meant it.

She continued playing with the grass, then after a while, "Greer, I like that name."

He stubbed his cigarette out now, cleared his throat. "Caroline. Me, too." His stomach felt queasy. He licked his lips, darted his eyes from side to side.

"You're always looking around," she said. "Don't you want to look at me?"

Greer made his eyes settle on her. It felt illegal to even gaze upon her. Boys like him had been killed for less.

"I don't feel alone right now," she said. "With you, I mean."

Greer was intensely aware of her presence, right down to noticing the small mole on her earlobe, the slip of her neckline, the bare skin where her locket had been. He agreed—he was most definitely not alone.

Caroline gave him a little tap. "Come on, say something nice or something. You're making me feel silly, doing all the talking. A line of poetry maybe?"

Greer gave a nervous laugh. "I'm having trouble thinking right now."

She nodded. "Yeah."

His throat felt so tight he didn't know if he could push any more words out. He searched his mind for something to say. The smell in the air—was it honeysuckle? The river? Her? It was intoxicating. "'If strangers meet,'" he said, finally alighting on a poem. He let himself look in her eyes for a second. Blue enough to drown in. "Know that one?"

"Wait, don't tell me," she said, her eyebrows knitting together for a second, then relaxing. "E.E. Cummings."

Greer smiled. "Yeah. That's it."

"It's not just if strangers meet," she said. "He talks about if strangers touch, too."

Greer felt his chest freeze up again. They stared at each other, the words hanging in the air. The dare.

She walked her fingers through the grass towards his and stopped just before she reached his hand. She looked up again, her eyes curious and fierce at the same time.

If strangers touch.

They were close. So close. Was the other leaning in, too? Yes. The tentacle of fear, but also the thrill. Contact. Sparks. A million butterflies flapping wings in his gut. Was it possible for the heart to beat everywhere at once?

His first kiss, but he caught on quick to that, too.

*   *   *

The next night, they got to kissing a lot sooner. The smell he'd noticed? It wasn't honeysuckle. It was her; everything was her.

Caroline told him sometimes she wished she were a boy—they were free, got to do anything they wanted.

"I'm glad you're a girl," Greer said. She was free to do whatever she wanted with him.

*   *   *

On the fourth night, Greer brought her a poem he'd copied out longhand from one of his books. She asked him to read it aloud and he did, voice shaking. She took the paper from him.

"You think I walk in beauty?" she asked.

"'Like the night/Of cloudless climes and starry skies.'"

She folded the note and put it in the front pocket of her pink day dress for safekeeping. "You make me feel beautiful."

"You are," he said.

This time when they kissed, they kept going. Hands, tongue, skin, sweat. When her panties came off she looked nervous, but determined.

She had something for him, too.

*   *   *

He watched the white Thunderbird pull away, the headlights like glowing orbs, floating, ethereally displaced. When viewed from the side, they cast sharp, narrow beams of light, but they created more a sense of seeing than aiding actual sight, the amount of darkness surrounding them so much greater.

Caroline completed the U-turn and the back of the car now faced him, red brake lights replacing the tiny orbs. They appeared, disappeared, then finally grew distant until swallowed by the night. Caroline had a lighted path for her return; Greer would have to stumble home with only what the stars and moon could offer, which wasn't much, here under the thick forest cover.

He didn't need light to guide him home, he decided. This he had learned about sight tonight, too; sight alone couldn't lead you in the right direction. You could roll your eyes over every inch of a thing and not extract any real meaning from what you saw. Caroline had physical beauty enough to spare, but she had something more. Magic.

Greer followed the banks of the river until it wound its way to East Bannen.

Bannen. How would Bannen contain him tonight, he who felt so free? He noticed everything and nothing on his way home; every sense felt alive, his whole being saturated with Caroline. This secret knowledge they had shared—he felt liberated and dangerous.

Greer was coming up on the path behind Wilson's when he started slowing down. He would have to calm this burning somehow. How would he hide that his whole self was aflame? He rounded the corner and started walking down Main Street, half expecting that the fire he emitted would wake the town, that people would fling open their shutters and exclaim at the brightness walking down the road in his form.

No one looked, however; there was no witness to his heat. The only person he saw on his way was Esse, standing on her porch and looking up at the stars again. He had noticed her doing this a lot lately; she looked so displaced, so lost. There was something almost dead about the unflinching way she stared at the sky. Whatever eccentricities she displayed, however, could be forgiven. She was no more than a child holding a child. Only eleven and no one knew how it'd come to pass.

Greer stood outside his door now and gathered himself to enter. He always felt he had to make himself small in this house, and he felt too big tonight.

The door creaked as he opened it. His mother wasn't in the front room. He was relieved, hoped he could make it to his room and guard his wildness there. Just as he was easing the front door shut, Elizabeth padded into the living room, her slippers muffling her footsteps.

"It's late," she said.

"Yeah, isn't it a beautiful night?"

"You know I worry about you."

"Mama, you know there's nothing to worry about out there. We're in little old Bannen."

"A place doesn't have to be big for meanness to set itself down on you."

Greer was too happy to hear words like meanness tonight, too happy to feel guilty that she had stayed up again waiting for him.

"Remember how you sang that one time, Mama? Don't you think a night like this deserves a song?" He walked into the kitchen to get some water. He was thirsty, maybe thirstier than he'd ever been before. "I don't want to live afraid of what *might* happen," he said, because his mother hadn't answered him, hadn't said anything.

"A little bit of fear protects you. There are some things you should be afraid of," Elizabeth said from behind him, following him into the kitchen.

Greer drank the water in one gulp then placed the glass back down. He turned to look at his mother whose face was drawn from lack of sleep. He wanted to tell her how much you miss if you always stay protected, closed off; nothing alive seeps in. He wanted to tell her about Caroline because keeping his elation inside almost hurt; he was too full with it, he would burst. He felt it rising in him again, wondered if he would start glowing, if his mother would notice how big and bright he was. He knew he couldn't tell her, though. He knew he couldn't tell anyone.

"I want to do more than just be safe, Mama. I want to do more than just survive. I want to live," Greer said.

Elizabeth rested her hands on the back of the chair, which stood at an awkward angle, not completely pushed in underneath the table. Greer wondered what she thought about what he'd just said. Seemed it was all she did—survive.

"Didn't you ever have a time when you felt free, Mama? Haven't you ever just spent a perfect day where you felt you lived a whole life—a great one?"

Elizabeth didn't say anything, only got that blank look on her face she always got when he asked her anything real, anything that mattered. He looked at this sad woman before him; it was hard to conjure up an image of her that might mirror what he had felt tonight with Caroline. "You make me feel whole," she'd said.

"Did my father make you feel alive, Mama?" he said quietly.

It was hardly noticeable, but he noticed, how she gripped the top of the chair with her hands.

"I told you, we never speak of the dead."

"And that's all you've ever told me. Shouldn't there be some joy we can talk about? Can't you ever say anything more than that?"

Elizabeth turned her head and gazed out the window.

"Is it fair? That's all you'll let him be? A drowned man. Wasn't he more than that?" Greer insisted.

"Don't talk about it," Elizabeth said loudly. "I don't want to talk about it," she said lowering her voice again.

"There are things *I* want, Mama. Don't you see I'm suffocating here? Why do you think I go out all the time? I don't mean to worry you, Mama, I really don't, but I can't stay here. I can't stay cooped up in here, never saying anything, never being able to ask anything."

Elizabeth had her back turned to him now, her arms folded across her chest. He was talking to her back now.

"I feel things sometimes," he said, talking slowly, not sure where the words were coming from, if maybe the freedom, unleashed and dangerous, was talking. "I feel like there are things we don't say that should be said. I feel like there's got to be more, and you don't say it. I'm almost sixteen, Mama. I'm trying to be a man. All I want to know is something about what kind of man my father was. Don't you think I deserve that much?" Greer turned back to the sink now, the two of them standing in the kitchen facing away from each other, Greer his head down, watching the tiny drops of water inching towards the drain, Elizabeth holding herself like she might fall down if she didn't.

"Sometimes I think he must still be out there," Greer said. "I don't believe you. I don't believe you sometimes."

He turned around and walked past his mother who still stood with her arms crossed tight across her chest. If he had stayed a moment longer, looked closely as he brushed past her, he would have seen her eyes growing moist. He didn't see, though, not the tears gathering in the corners of her eyes, or that slight bit of energy a body gathers right before speaking.

*   *   *

Greer stood out on the porch for a long time that night, filling his lungs, which just a few hours ago had been at the ready to shout Caroline's name into the night. He had wanted to whoop, call out into the woods that he was on top of the world. Now he felt defeated.

The seeing doesn't matter, he told himself. That's what he's learned, isn't it? How was it possible, even after everything that had happened tonight, that he'd still come back to this yearning? Missing some person he'd never seen, someone he'd never known.

Greer placed his hands on the railing as if bracing himself. He passed over scenes of the love of this evening and wondered about the unknown past. Was he created in love? He saw very little in his mind: dark shadows, white space.

It was very late by now, and the evening cool. It was his turn to cross his arms around himself. His fire had died down. The night stood pitch black. No one would mistake him for a flame now. Only a restless boy searching for someone he wouldn't know even if they stood right in front of him.

FIVE

(1977)

Whenever Greer left his mother's house now, Ceiley always seemed to be there. It's not that she waited for him—though he couldn't be sure she didn't. He didn't mind—she was actually the easiest person to talk to since he'd returned. She'd tag along with whatever errand he was doing, or they'd go down to Snake Creek to get away for a little while.

Greer offered Ceiley the stories she liked best—descriptions of people and places she could barely imagine, only a few she'd seen in books. Women who could carry anything on their head, from large pails of water to long stalks of wheat. Men who wore dresses and bundles of cloth like beehives on top. Churches with a thousand spires, paintings made of sand.

Greer grew to enjoy telling these tales. It was like a catalogue of what he'd seen, only the good parts. Giving her a snapshot of the world outside Bannen seemed one of the saving graces of coming back here. It reminded him, too, that he had managed to get out, even if he was back here now. Since that day when the caged bird flew away, it was like they had some unspoken sympathy, the siren song of escape calling them at the same time.

As they threw rocks into Sicama River he took her down the Nile. "You pass pyramids and villages and travel from one civilization to the next." With only the woods watching, he described the Seine in the center of a city, great stone bridges crossing from one bank to the other. Ceiley liked the thought of a City of Light. He could almost see what she must imagine: illuminated streets, everyone and everything shimmering, twinkling. What was it like to live in a place where everything glowed?

Greer didn't tell her everything, though. That at this same Seine he had seen police push hundreds of men as dark as him into its waters. That some of the villages by the banks of a river in Africa were little more than straw—and they were the lucky ones. At least they had water.

Greer heard of the tumult back home, too, watched on grainy TV screens men and women felled by fire hoses, beaten bloody in marches, taunted at lunch counters, chased by fierce dogs. As he moved about the world he saw the different ways man removes himself from himself. If anyone asked why he had left, he would not tell them his personal tale, and he certainly wasn't going to tell Ceiley. His story seemed too small in comparison. Who was he to say that the wars outside mirrored one within? Who was he, but nobody?

*　　　*　　　*

Nowhere in East Bannen was markedly better off than the other parts, but there were a couple streets that seemed even poorer than the rest. Little Egypt was where all the shoddiest shotgun houses stood. No one remembered how it came to be called that, Little Egypt. There wasn't anybody who'd been to the actual country and there was no obvious resemblance as far as Greer could tell.

The road was especially muddy today after a hard afternoon rain. Ditches overflowed with brown water. The soggy surroundings made everything look more limp and desperate than usual.

Greer was walking along, surveying the houses on cinderblocks and sagging crates. So at odds with their namesake. What of pharaohs or the Sahara, pyramids and kings?

Still, he almost preferred this part of town to his street. He even had a theory for why. A fired bullet in a shotgun house could sail straight from the front room to the back; that's supposedly how they got that name. Ghosts were said to like these houses because they could easily pass through, too. The people living in these spaces might not like this, but the spirits sure did.

Could this explain his draw to these sad little houses? he wondered. He, who felt like a ghost? His history haunted him. It hollowed him out.

A few people were out on the porches, gabbing back and forth, but most were huddled inside since the wood exteriors were still wet. Those who were out gave a perfunctory wave if he caught their eye, but they returned just as fast to their talk.

A small child played in the yard a few houses up. Just a toddler, Greer couldn't tell whether it was a boy or girl from here. The wire grass had been pummeled flat by the storm; the child seemed absorbed with whatever was crawling around on the ground. Maybe a snail leaving its silvery trail. Or big Palmetto bugs that always appeared after the rain.

The child started chasing something, wobbly on stubby legs, then tripped over a tire in the yard and fell forward into its hole.

No one else had taken notice yet, not even the ladies, the child's kin, sitting on the porch. Greer ran toward the toddler, hopped over the low-hanging fence. He swooped the child up safe into his arms. He could see now the tire held a reservoir of water. The little boy had fallen face down into the puddle and hadn't been able to right himself up.

"My goodness!" the ladies said now, coming to meet him. Greer patted the boy on the back. He sputtered, then went silent for a sharp moment. Then he started wailing. That was a relief.

"Oh Sugar, Big Tee," said a large woman, holding out her arms for the child. The child leaned towards her and Greer passed him over.

"Tell Grandma what happened," she said over the loud crying.

"He fell into that puddle," Greer said.

"Did you fall down, Sugar?" the woman cooed at the child.

"He could have drowned that way," Greer said.

"Oh, sweet Jesus," the woman said.

The child continued to cry, more scared than anything now.

The woman looked at Greer. "You Miss Elizabeth's boy?"

"Yeah," Greer said.

"Heard tell you were back in town. Good man, thank you."

Greer flushed. "Just reflex," he said.

"It's all right, Sugar," the grandmother said to the child, turning to bring him inside.

"Tell your mama hey," called out the woman before disappearing, and Greer said, "Will do," even though he could no longer remember her name.

He left the yard and continued walking on his way. It wasn't until he was another block ahead that it started catching up to him. He was already out of Little Egypt by the time he paused to sit down.

It had only been a few seconds. It's not like the boy had really been about to drown. But what if he *hadn't* gotten to him, Greer thought. Accidents like that happen all the time.

Greer realized he was holding all his muscles tight, even holding his breath. He sat there, and just tried to relax again. He felt shaky, wished he had a cigarette. It was rare, but there were a few times in life he did feel human. This might be one of them.

Greer got up again, started walking toward home, the shotgun houses now replaced with modest bungalows.

The curse of the ghost is that he's forever trapped in one moment, the one his soul cannot get past. Greer had broken out of this cycle at times, seen glory, seen light. But whatever else he experienced, no matter how many miles he'd traveled, his mind would inevitably return here. A boy of sixteen, first learning the cruelty of the world. He might wear the shell of a man, but he didn't always feel like one.

AKUA GLORIA APPIAH

(1973-1977)

Wen a bone breaks, you have to reset it. It grows back on its own if nothing is done, but it will be misaligned, damaged in the nerves, possibly infected.

I wonder if it is the same for people. They break, put the pieces back together best they can, but they are never the same. And what about the heart?

We have a saying where I come from in Ghana, "One who can speak never goes missing." Greer did not want to be a man who leaves, but it is hard to battle one's history. There are some things Greer could never say aloud; it is what kept him fully from me.

In the hospital ward, I saw many bad things; things we could not fix because we did not have the medicine, the equipment. But I know there are invisible scars, too. The bruised spirit does not always have the strength to speak, but it is far worse than any flesh wound, than any disease. My people told me I was chosen to heal. I went to school, educated myself so that I could fulfill this mission. But a woman with a man is someone else. If he comes to you broken, you can try, but there is no use crying if you cannot put him back together again.

Once, Greer told me about his journey to Paris when he first arrived in Europe. He walked over uneven cobblestones, noticed how tall iron streetlamps cut shadows with their glowing orbs. The way he spoke made pictures in my head. Grey drizzle left the streets, the stones, wet, covered everything in rain. The city was like a frozen fire, he said. Cold, distant, yet illuminated at a thousand watts.

He was like that, too. My frozen fire. We would get so close, we could no longer tell whose breath was whose, but some part of him was always far away. Even when we made love, I could not tell if he was with me. He was generous, gave me pleasure—oh! how I moaned—but the way he moved over me, the almost vacant look in his eyes, I could not read his spirit. What did he feel? He told me he was a ghost.

Kweku. Born on a Wednesday. In Akan, we all have such a name. I am *Akua*, Akua Gloria, also born on Wednesday, the female form. I called him Kweku when we were alone. He said the word sounded like "quake." An earthquake. He was not only frozen fire; he had hot lava inside. He was a volcano, too. Only when we were alone. "I've been dormant for years," he said. I awakened him.

We met on the great boat where he worked. I was leaving from Accra for the first time, going on a big metal ship so heavy it should have fallen to the bottom of the ocean. London, I was going to London, where the power of the pound was said to be mighty. Where my brothers had gone, where family could welcome me. We have family everywhere.

This is what I tried to teach him. He did not know about family. He did not understand our ways. When he asked, "But how could you leave your daughter?" I said, "But it is for her that I left. She has her grandmother, her aunties—Auntie Araba is her favourite. I go so she can have a better life."

Soon he did not judge me. He saw it was true what we say: "The family is like the forest. If you are outside, it is dense. If you are inside, you see that each tree has its own position."

With my brothers and cousins and the other Ghanaians in our small flat in Brixton we shared everything. We would eat *fufu* together, all from the same bowl. With our hands. The palm oil we used tasted bitter to him at first, the red too much the colour of blood. But he learned that, too, that his tastes could change. "I can change, I can change," he said in a corner sometimes, so quietly he thought I could not hear.

He had voices inside him, other words he did not speak. They burned there like his goodness burned. I was drawn to his light. Kweku Greer. He did not draw attention to himself, but he did not have to. He was as bright as the batik I wore, that I would soon find stood out too much against the grey London sky. A nurse like me was to wear white. My colourful stripes on hand-made cloth were not welcome in the city of concrete, whose sky was not blue. I did not find work as a nurse in London as I thought I would, but as a cleaner. I told him, it does not matter the name of the work that we do. I make money to send my daughter, to pay her school fees. What matters is love and family.

On the boat, we began to talk, shyly at first. He said with mostly men on the freighters, with being out to sea all the time, he had almost forgotten how to speak to a woman. "We have our transistor radios, we play cards, see how far we can spit. It's not a place for a woman," he said.

I asked him, did he have a different woman in each port? He said he did not. I believed him. That is not to say he did not ever have any woman before me. I could feel, the way he ran his light hands over my body, his touch, he had laid down before. I could imagine, my Kweku—always kind, never cruel—that women had always wanted him.

He carried too much. He liked my proverbs, always wanted to hear more. "No one tests the depth of the river with both feet," I said.

"And another?" he asked.

"Do not call the forest that shelters you a jungle."

He had what we might call proverbs, too. Poems. I did not always understand them, but I saw they worked in the same way for him. And music. I still laugh to think of it. When we first met, he mentioned a song called "Gloria" which I had not heard. "On the B-side," he said. "Of 'Baby, please don't go.'" Again, I did not understand. There were things we did not understand about each other, but I think that is why we liked each other, too. "I could get lost in you," he said, finally, after a few years. He must have thought this was a good thing, the way he said it. I did not know that being lost could approach happiness, but I was happy if he should be lost in a way he liked. Sometimes, he was just lost.

I did not see him often at first, as he was always on that great ship, coming or going. But when I told him on the next time, that I would return to Ghana, that Ewurama had had her first blood and I wanted to see her now that she was a woman, he surprised me and said he would like to see my home.

I think he was searching, always searching, and wondered if he might find peace there with me. The bright sun of Ghana did revive him in a way; it brought back some of his words. He said the heat smelled different here. He talked about Georgia and of the humidity and of a thick swamp. He talked of the different heaviness of heat, how he preferred the breeze that came from Cape Coast to that of Bannen. It was the first time he had spoken of that place. It was like he had been born on the ocean and nothing had come before. We heard only of America. But Bannen was his village.

A hundred times a day people would call out to him: "*Broyni!* White man!" He cared for us, but I could see the hurt in his eye when they said this. I told him it was just our word, for any light-skinned foreigner. It means "person from behind the horizon."

From Ola Heights, I had grown up with a view of the sea. But we did not go down there; it was dangerous and dirty on the beach. People who did not have homes (oh! Who would leave relatives without shelter?) would sleep there at night. But Kweku Greer liked the sea. After two times on the ship, I could see there was another way to hold the sea.

Ewurama liked him. He liked Ewurama. He would be a good father. I told him, "You are a father. Look at Ewurama." But his eyes were sad. I knew what he thought: *She is not really mine.* Oh! But with love such a thing does not matter.

She was too big to lift on his shoulders when we came, but they played other games. They raced each other between the palm tree and the log, or between Kofi's tire shop and our house, kicking up dirt along the way.

But I knew he was not meant to be here. *It is the calm and silent water that drowns a man.* This is another one of our sayings, but I did not say it to him.

He told me once, when it was time to discuss shame, that bad things happened when he was around. That his love turned things to poison.

I told him, "Kweku, Kweku Greer, you are a good man. Do not speak like that."

But I saw the time come when he could learn this lesson. He received a paper with a photo of a river on one side, and words on the other from a Reverend Smith. It talked of his mother. He never talked about his mother. And I said, "This is the sickness that you carry. Where is your family? You left home, you must go home to your family."

He tossed several nights in a row. He did not want to go. But he woke up early one day and said, yes, he would go. He said, "The shame. I never really told you."

I said, "Kweku Greer, your soul has told me everything."

If you are on a road to nowhere, find another road. It was not by staying with us that the faraway look in his eyes would disappear into the night.

I loved him, so I released him. We do not say goodbye here. We say, "We shall meet."

He told me then, when he thought of me, he would not think of that song he had first sung—or even that new one that arrived just as we were leaving London, spelling my name. He thought instead of a choir. Gloria in excelsis. He said, "Gloria. Glory to Thee who has shown me the light."

I said, "It is about God."

"Yes. But I thank you, Gloria, for your light."

I hope he shines bright in Bannen, that place where he went back to. I told him, "You do not need to worry about me. Go and find your family." My first husband I buried. Greer is still alive in the world. I did not have to bury him. "Whenever we dig may it become a well full of water." This is the last proverb I wanted to leave him with.

We dig so that we might find water, Kweku. When we drink out of the well, we find health and strength.

He wanted to leave me with Gloria, glory. Glory unto the light.

My light. His light. Even if we never see each other again, I say, we shall meet.

SIX

(1977)

Ceiley and Greer were down by the river, skipping stones
along the water. It was hot. Ceiley's jeans were rolled up
to her knees and a white T-shirt was acquiring smudges.
She was examining each rock, wondering which kind they
corresponded to: quartz, staurolite, feldspar. She liked saying
these names, even though she couldn't identify them yet. Greer
was smoking a cigarette with his left hand so he could throw the
rocks with his right.

"I had to fill out these stupid forms for school today,"
Ceiley said.

"Oh yeah, why were they stupid," he said. Another funny
thing about Greer, she thought: He seemed curious, wanted to
know things, yet it always sounded like he already kind of knew
the answers. His voice didn't hint at question marks.

Ceiley leaned down and picked up another rock. "It
should be a lot easier, you know. Parents' information. Names,
dates, occupation. Dead, alive. No, no, but not for me."

"Your mom," he said, blowing smoke out of the side of his
mouth.

"Yeah," she said, tossing a stone, not even attempting to
make it bounce on the water. "Well at least I'm the one who

fills them out now, not her. She always complained there was no place for the divine in what I'm learning. Like, yeah, Mama. There's no box for 'child of God.'"

Greer laughed small, a tinny sound. Not as warm as she had grown accustomed to.

"She's right, though," she said. "Some other options might be good. Like 'delusional.'"

Greer took a long drag on his cigarette and lifted his head as he released a gray cloud of smoke up to the heavens.

"You know, Ceiley, I think maybe people just need to create their own story sometimes. Name their own origins."

Origins. He always used words like that—simple, yet vibrating with intensity.

"You're from here, right?" she said after a pause.

"Yeah," he said.

"So, are you leaving again soon?" She had been thinking about this. It had become as big a part of her routine as going to church this past month—walking to Wilson's, talking to Greer as he steadied his bicycle, listening to all the wonders of the world he'd recount as she tried to imagine such wild and precious things.

"I don't know yet. Maybe. But I've got to know about my mother first. What's going on." He ashed into the water.

"Anyway, my mama said you were gone there for a long time."

"Yeah," he said absently.

"I want to come with you…the next time you go, I mean."

Greer's hand lifting the cigarette to his mouth stopped halfway, then continued. "No…no," he said slowly. "That's not going to work, Ceiley."

"Why not?" she said, trying to control the tremor in her voice.

"There's no need to rush out there, kid. It's not always so great." Greer snuffed out his cigarette and drew another stone from his pocket. He watched it bounce two, three times, and kept looking at the surface of the water even after the last ripple had faded. "You're smart, you'll get out of here, Ceiley." He paused. "Ceiley—what's that from anyway? Celeste?"

"Celestial." Ceiley's cheeks got hot. She didn't usually go around telling people that—so embarrassing. There were things she kept telling Greer, though. Confiding things she hadn't named secrets but realized were once she had released them, feeling how close in she had kept them.

"Mmm, of course," he ruminated on it in his way. "'There was a time when meadow, grove and stream/ The earth, and every common sight/ To me did seem Apparell'd in celestial light/ The glory and the freshness of a dream.'"

Ceiley hoped he was onto one of his soliloquies. The kind she tried to still her breathing for, to make sure he stopped noticing she was there, so he would just keep talking. That month, he'd told her about street hawkers in Algiers and a Spanish city containing mountains and sea both. He could speak in tongues, not like the ladies at revival, but in ones that sounded like soft lullabies or words formed from flowing water.

Greer didn't keep talking, though. He just skipped another stone.

She returned to the issue at hand. "You don't like it here, either. Don't you want to go?" She didn't dare say "together," to risk it again, though there seemed no separation between the pulsing of this wish and her heartbeat. When he didn't say anything right away, she added quickly, "You already did it once. You know how."

Greer's face washed over with a look, nearly blank, but pained. "You're a sweet kid."

Her palms felt sweaty, her mouth dry. She seemed able to hear every movement of her body suddenly: her eyelids opening and closing, her breath coming in and out.

"You remind me of a girl in Ghana. So full of life and curiosity. She's about your age, too."

That made her a little jealous, but the idea that she could resemble someone that far away, from a different world for all she knew—she did like that. She liked much less what he said next: "Ewurama. She was almost like a daughter to me."

Ceiley didn't say anything, letting the information sink in. Then, "Ewurama? What kind of stupid name is Ewurama?" She said that, instead of the other, real thing ricocheting within: *A daughter? That's how you think of me?*

He smiled at her, that warm parting of lips that she loved, but right now hated.

"Ceiley, I'm just an old man," he said, as if he could read her thoughts, trying to be funny. "You're going to break boys' hearts one day. I promise."

She threw a rock into the river, then another, then another, as she willed the tears starting to well up in her eyes to stay right where they were.

oo o

oo o

o o o

oo o

o o o

Ceiley arranged the peas in the formation she had seen in the math textbook. Fifteen, a hexagonal polygonal, a rhombic dodecahedral, could be partitioned in 176 ways. She told herself to take a lesson from this—so many different options deriving from a few. She was fifteen. Time to explore some other possibilities.

"Girl, when are you going to learn some manners? Why are you always playing with your food?" Esse asked.

Ceiley kept pushing the peas across the plate. They had never been her favorite, these wrinkled, squishy little things.

"Heavens above, I do not know what goes through your head, child. I really don't," Esse said, snatching the plate from Ceiley, wresting away her utensils.

Ceiley thought that was probably one of the truest things her mother had said in a long time. Her mother *didn't* have any idea what went on in her head. The numbers, the words. Anything concrete, based in fact, facts that she could not rely on finding in this house of stargazing and Bible nights. This house where things did not add up.

Without preamble Ceiley just asked. "Is Greer my father?"

Esse's jaw dropped open and she looked like someone had shot her with a stun gun, the way she froze with that expression on her face. She reminded Ceiley of a blowfish with her mouth just hanging in that ugly "o."

"Well?"

Esse was shaking her head. "What kind of fool notion is that?" she said, finally finding some words.

"He treats me like that. You don't like him much." Ceiley sat slumped over the table, sullen, miserable.

"I don't know what's gotten into you lately, Miss Thing, but Greer ain't your daddy."

Ceiley let that settle. Considering the thoughts she'd had about him, she was relieved, though some other part of her, strange as it seemed, also felt disappointed.

"The only Father you have to worry about is the one up there," Esse was saying, pointing her finger to the ceiling. "How many times I got to tell you?"

"You're crazy," she muttered under her breath.

"What's that? You talking back again?"

"I'm just talking," Ceiley said louder. "You call *me* a fool? No one believes you and your crazy stories."

Ceiley didn't see it coming. As disapproving as her mother could be, she rarely got rough with her. The slap made a sickening sound, knocked Ceiley's head hard to the side. Tears sprang to her eyes, but she wasn't crying. She was angry.

She put her hand on her left cheek, right over the sting. She glared at Esse, who looked more upset than she did now.

"I'm too old to be smacking around," she said and got up calmly this time, walked out the door. Even if she'd heard her mother say she was sorry, it wouldn't have mattered one bit.

* * *

Ceiley had one refuge in town, and that was the library. Not that Bannen had much of one to speak of. Like Wilson's, it was an affair lacking in variety, mainly with holdings from the collection of Don and Marie Thompson. A library dependent on one couple's books made for a skewed sample, their peculiarities evident as selections on Egyptian mummification or the history of Gullah on the Sea Islands lined the wood bookcases, but maps or links to the contemporary world could barely be found. Still, Ceiley felt it was the one place where she belonged in Bannen, she the library's most devoted patron. She learned what she could from their catalogue, but it was proving useless for her next project.

Without access to an atlas, Ceiley had been trying for
the past week to gain information from Greer about the places
he'd traveled. She put on her brave face, acted like he hadn't
broken her heart. She didn't want to be too obvious, but she
needed names, she needed routes. Did he have an old compass
that showed true north? And surely one couldn't get very far
on a bicycle, right? Would a thumb in the air suffice to stop a
vehicle willing to transport a young girl to a place unknown but
imagined?

If he didn't want to take her, fine, she'd show him—she'd
show *everyone*—and go herself.

It was July, not even the nights a respite from the
humidity and the mosquitoes that clamored in the wet air.
Ceiley stood on the porch, the murmur of her mother's prayers
seeping through the screen door. She gazed up, unable to focus
on any one thing, only noticing the odd green tint of the sky.
Her stomach felt like it was rolling in on itself, as if she hadn't
eaten anything for dinner. Any grand gesture requires some
boldness, she thought.

She waited until her mother's prayers subsided, snores
taking their place, then went back inside to collect her small
bag. She held the screen door as it closed, to make sure it didn't
make a sound. She headed towards the river, which she had
settled on as her first guide. She remembered the many slave
narratives in the Thompson collection, that many people on the
escape followed a river—if worse came to worst, they ducked
under the water to escape notice when they heard passersby.

Greer had taught her about how water flows, the anomaly
of Bannen's river that had its own directional pull, seemingly
against the dictates of physics. To every rule there is an
exception, he had said. He had made his own rules, seemed to
Ceiley, and now she'd make hers. She didn't have much to go on
as far as destination, but north seemed the safest bet for now.

Air was cooler the farther up you went, and if nothing else, the compass' arrow would always point there.

*   *   *

As Ceiley was looking up and following the river's flow, Greer was in Bannen, listening to his mother's labored breathing and watching the faded pink curtain fluttering in the window, catching glimpses of the strange green sky outside. He did not read renewal in the pocket of sky he saw now. He pictured the tissue in Elizabeth's chest as this pestilent green. She continued her refusal to go to the hospital, as if not saying anything about her sickness could stop it, but he knew: the cancer was killing her.

He looked at Elizabeth, whose eyes even when closed reminded him of the line on the horizon where you stopped being able to see what lay beyond. As endless as ocean, though he had said this to her once when he was young and she didn't take it well: "my two worst moments saw me covered in water."

Greer nodded off, as if carried by waves, only to start awake to a loud knock at the door, an urgent, repeated "Hello" carrying into the bedroom, a demand more than a question. He shook his head, glanced at the clock on the nightstand table. 3:15 a.m. He approached the door and saw Esse's damp face through the mesh.

"Where's my baby?" she said. "What have you done with my baby?"

"Let's slow down," Greer said, opening the door to let her pass through.

"She hasn't come back tonight. Look at the time. What's a baby girl doing out at this time?"

Greer poured Esse some water from a jug sitting on the living room table. The basic questions didn't need to be asked, the situation clear. Even so, he asked them from the beginning, giving himself time to shake off the unfit sleep, and Esse a chance to calm down.

"Ok, I'll go look for her. If you could stay with my mother. She's not doing well."

"You," Esse said, pointing, "what makes you think I'd let you go alone? You're the cause of this. Before she met you…"

"Before me what?" Greer said, his voice pitching louder, but steady.

"Before you, there wouldn't be a right now. She wouldn't be out there at all." Esse was shaking, her arms folded across her lap, hugging herself so tightly as if she were trying to reach through her body.

"Blame is a funny thing," Greer said. "You think it will make you feel better, but it doesn't."

"Don't you tell me nothing about blame. I know when to wield it, and when to look to the invisible. You I see. Don't you tell me nothing about blame."

A clock ticked loudly in the hallway.

"Look, we're both concerned about Ceiley right now and that's what we need to focus on. I have a good idea of what she's up to. You can trust me."

Esse shook her head, trying to shake the headache out, stop the vice from closing in around her skull.

"It's not something I take lightly, ok?" Greer said. It was not something he tossed around, trust. It was too fragile for that.

"Where is she?" she asked, a pleading in her voice.

"I think she's probably down by the river."

Esse's eyes widened.

"I don't know much about what's been going on here, Esse. I've tried to forget everything I ever knew about Bannen. But you know I'm not like that," he said, picking up his pack of cigarettes on the side table and lighting one. "Something happened to you down there, even if no one ever talked about it. God, no one talks about anything around here," he said, pushing an angry cloud of smoke out of his mouth, aware of his mother, lying troubled in the next room.

Esse's eyes seemed to glaze over. She sat rigid, her spine unbending. She didn't respond, like she had cotton in her ears.

"That girl of yours is a headstrong one," Greer said, looking at her again, taking a deep inhale that seemed to refocus him, soften his voice. "Not a bad trait, really," he said. "Don't worry, I'll find her," he said, trying to offer a reassuring smile. He brought the cigarette to his lips when he couldn't muster it.

"Just get out of here," Esse said, sounding so tired suddenly. Rustlings from the other room floated into the den, Elizabeth shifting in bed. "But man, you're going to come back. Man, bring my baby back to me safe."

*   *   *

Just a few miles out of town, where the tobacco fields began their ascension, Ceiley stopped and sat down by the bank, disconcerted by all the night sounds she had never noticed before, the intense darkness when only fireflies provide light, the last lamp many houses ago. The water was black, the sky moonless. A warm breeze enveloped her, but she shivered nonetheless.

To still the encroaching fear, drown out the coming doubt, Ceiley computed equations, recited sonnets, thought of Greer. Which way was north? Taking out the rusty compass, she stared at its face, inscrutable in the dark. A sign, a shooting star—god, all her heated distaste for her mother's antics and here she was looking for the same things. Esse had sung praises when Ceiley was born a Virgo, the virgin, her symbol. She conceded the date fell on the cusp, however, with all the dramatic qualities of a lion Leo a possibility. With boldness shrinking in the night, Ceiley felt her leonine tendencies receding back into the interior spaces where she kept her unspoken voice. She only hoped daybreak could call back her true intentions.

Ceiley curled up on a lonely patch of ground. She cried. She slept.

*   *   *

Her eyes flew open only to meet solid black so dense she might have kept them closed for all the help they provided. She turned quickly onto her stomach, this seeming a better defensive position—on your back the heart too open to the world. She continued trying to regain her sight against the inky darkness, cursing the sense that functioned now, the wrong one, too acute. Who was there? What? A noise approaching, fading, everywhere, ether.

"Celestial."

Ceiley yelped, the voice suddenly upon her, a hand on her, too.

"God," she said, her eyes adjusting to the light, "Greer."

"What's up?" he said.

"Nothing much," she said, trying to regain some composure.

"That so," Greer said. "I'd say a lot's up. I'd say, maybe you should get up." He drew a pack of Camels out of his pocket and motioned to her.

Ceiley stumbled to her feet, wobblier than she would have hoped, clutching the rusty compass in her right hand. Standing before him, as always, awkward, thrilled. *Thank you,* she mouthed to the river, before looking up at him.

"Kid, you've done a number." He lit a cigarette with his silver lighter. "You didn't have to run away so quick, you know. I didn't think you were actually going like that."

"I just had to get out, you know?"

Greer nodded, sucked on his cigarette. He kept looking at her, blowing smoke rings, so she kept talking.

"I," she began, "it's just that, you said I couldn't go with you. You said it wasn't time. I'm tired of people deciding things for me."

"Yeah, like what kinds of things?"

"Like where I have to be every day. Like honor thy parents, even if they're crazy. Like who I can spend my time with." She looked at him. "Like having to believe in fairy tales."

"Hate to break it to you, but you are fifteen."

"See, and I hate that, too. Like I don't know anything. Like I'm a baby. My mama had me when she was younger than me. Oh, I'm sorry, I *appeared* to my holy virgin mother."

Greer considered this, then gave a little nod. "You're right. I'm sorry. I always hated that, too." He blew out a torrent of smoke. "I didn't tell you, I was a little older than you when I headed out."

"Yeah?" Ceiley tried to lower her voice, so as not to seem too eager. Whereas Greer's voice was steady, hers was always up in the clouds, way too high when she was around him. Sounded like shrieking in her ears.

"Yeah, I was just turning sixteen. People *weren't* telling me some things. That's what got to me." He threw his cigarette to the ground and stepped on it.

Edges were beginning to lighten, the day announcing its impending arrival. They began walking, Ceiley trying not to ask too many direct questions about this new revelation. Greer let his stories slip slowly, in measured meters.

"Where did you learn to speak in poetry?" she asked instead.

"What?" Greer glanced over at her without breaking stride.

"Celestial light, fresh dreams, green meadows—that sort of thing. People don't really talk like that."

"Yeah, I know. I just started memorizing things. To fill the silence."

"Fill the silence? You could do that on your own, couldn't you?"

"Yes, yes I could. I should." They kept walking for awhile. "It's just that sometimes other people's words are so beautiful," Greer said, picking up like the silent moments hadn't passed, and as if they had. "It's exactly what you'd want to say, if you only thought of it. And sometimes words are ugly, lies, things intended to make you shut up, so you don't speak any of your own. I guess I've found it easier to rely on words that have already been tested."

"You've said some things to me I bet you made up on your own. At least, it seems like that."

He let out a long exhale. It was a relief. It was hard to breathe.

*   *   *

Early morning dawned over the hills, the green sky of the previous night giving way to soft, newborn pink, delivering a new day. They were approaching Bannen, the familiar chapel in view.

"Oh god, we're back here already."

"Where did you think we were going?"

"Nowhere," Ceiley said, stopping, kicking the dirt. She hadn't noticed till now. "Not yet, though. Please."

"All right," Greer said. "I know the feeling."

They walked closer to the water. "I didn't get very far, did I?" she said, slinking into the subtle slope of the river's bank. "I mean, I wanted to cross a state line, like you."

Greer sat down next to her. "Celestial"—only from him did the name sound right—"I'm not sure I'm the best model of what to do. You probably shouldn't be looking to follow in my footsteps."

"But there's got to be better than Bannen, right? I want to live some of your poems, your stories."

"I didn't complete all those stories, Ceiley. They're not always as good in reality as they are in the telling." Greer placed his palm on the grass and gathered several blades in a fist, tearing them from the roots. "You leave this town because you're angry, leave with unsettled business—believe me, you'll never really escape it."

Ceiley looked at Greer, whose eyes were growing watery in the day's approaching light.

"You know what the most fearless act is?" he said. "Even braver than running away?"

Ceiley shook her head.

"Facing it. What's before you, where you are. There are things to learn here," he said, speaking more slowly, more to himself now. "Hard to believe, I know, but I guess it's true," he said, still playing with the grass, letting out a resigned laugh. "You can't spend your whole life trying to start over. There's no use pining after things that are no longer green."

Ceiley looked at him for a moment; she could see this had nothing to do with her anymore. "What's that from?" she asked.

"Nothing," he said. "I just made it up."

They sat in silence and watched the sun come up over the creek, Ceiley calculating the distance between a heart's desire and Bannen's town limit, Greer letting his own words sink in. The first rays hit their faces.

DELIVERY

(1961)

Greer's eyes followed the familiar path as he walked along the bank of Snake Creek. It felt hotter than usual that day, even with the sun only raining down in patches through the leaves. Another box had arrived with no return address; stiff cardboard like the others, a single swatch of masking tape holding it shut. Greer had studied the careful script—seemingly written to be as nondescript as possible—but the evenly sketched letters revealed little other than the intended destination.

He ran a hand over his thick black hair, pondering the source of this latest package. It seemed impossible that these heavy boxes should appear so regularly as to be random.

The first one had arrived a few years ago, just as he was starting at the junior high school, still segregated four years after some high court ruled this unlawful; Bannen stood largely untouched by what might be called "national" news elsewhere. The town was local, and the biggest news in Greer's life till that point had been the sudden appearance of the anonymous box, him coming home to find his mother in the living room, hurriedly repacking its contents.

"What's this?" he had said.

"Nothing."

This was not true, of course. Such denials would cease to surprise him in the near future, but at the time, it still puzzled Greer how people contradicted the so clearly evident. Like here, the simple fact that there were twenty books strewn across the living room floor, his mother on hands and knees.

Greer reached down and picked up a book. *Leaves of Grass*.

"Where did these come from?" he asked.

"Nowhere."

Other than silence, this was typical of his mother's preferred mode of communication—short, negative responses.

"They came from somewhere. Let's have a look."

Elizabeth didn't reply, only hurled one book after the other into the box, hunching over it to block him from getting closer.

Greer, already bigger than his mother even then, knelt down next to her and pulled the box towards him, ignoring her protests and her hands, which slapped at his. He closed the box's flaps to look for an address; he found just his own and laughed.

"There's nothing funny here," Elizabeth said.

"I'm just laughing at the address, Mama. A name and our town, not even a street. We're so small anyone can find us. But who's looking?"

"No one," she said.

Greer decided to leave the questions behind for the moment, though the box only fed into his growing list, ones his mother never answered. He'd tried enough times to know she was never inclined to tell him much of anything.

Sometimes, Greer would listen for the sound of the house settling; something about a structure so solid and heavy still shifting, not being done with its movement, comforted him. Living within concrete walls where so few words were spoken made him uneasy. The books he discovered in the box that first night—he had found it in a corner under a faded piece of cloth, the house too small to conceal large objects, even if other things remained so—confirmed his feeling that there existed a lot more to say, many ways to say it. He had sat up long into a late hour, his light the only one left burning in Bannen, devouring words describing worlds far away. His mother had never denied him the books after that—finding him asleep the next day with his right hand still tucked into a volume of poetry, a placid, content expression on his face—but she always insisted on opening the box first. She told him to keep the fact of these deliveries to himself.

This time, she hadn't gotten to the box. She was out taking one of her solitary walks to wrestle what must have been demons. Greer had followed her once, to a small patch of forest where she sat at the base of a willow tree and rocked herself back and forth for several hours. He never wanted to be witness to that again.

For the first time since these boxes started appearing, Greer didn't immediately plunge into it, distracted by what lay on top.

Elizabeth:

For the boy, 16 years after that day.

And for you, silver.

J.T.

Greer turned the cream stationary over, checking if there might be more. A million questions unfurled themselves before him. Who could be addressing his mother this way? And "the boy?" Was he the boy? Obviously.

Greer stared at the note for a long time before folding it in two, almost sorry to put a crease in the paper, this evidence of...of what? He didn't even know what it was telling him.

He stuffed the note in his pocket, though he took it out almost immediately to read it again. He shook his head and glanced at the longcase clock, whose pendulum dutifully swung from one side to the other, the doleful ticking shaking him out of his stupor. He had never missed a date with Caroline, could never wait to see her, in fact, but he didn't much feel like going right now. He wanted to think, and he couldn't think straight around her. That, of course, was one of her charms—very little thinking was involved. If it were, he would come to the conclusion that meeting a white girl at the outskirts of town was too perilous to continue. He didn't want to reach that conclusion—she was the best thing he had.

He was on his way, already passing the curious bend in the creek where the bank abruptly turns from green grass to stone, when he realized he hadn't even investigated the rest of the box. Silver, the note had said. Greer stopped, turning back towards the house. There must be something other than the usual books in that box. And who was J.T.?

He stood just minutes away from the meeting place, the tall sweetgum tree he and Caroline called the "us shrub" in sight. Suddenly he felt indecisive about everything. Should he go tell Caroline what happened or just go back? They rarely talked of anything that would root them to the world outside the clearing. Most of the time, they had no town, no past, no family. It was better that way, they said; how else would they have found each other, if not by straying from home?

Still, when they weren't making out or trading names of exotic locales, Greer liked to hear what little information Caroline would offer of her life—"so pedestrian" she called it. He was always fascinated by the workings of real families, he who had only his mother. Caroline said he probably wasn't missing much, when he'd confided he wished he'd known his father; hers barely knew she was there. Greer said he always thought it strange; seemed *no one* ever knew his father before he died. It was as if he were a ghost.

He started running towards her, though he didn't know what he would explain when he reached her. *I'm onto something. Pieces are missing, but they're coming. I've always felt there was something more.*

Today she lay stretched out on a checkered blanket, her legs crossed one over the other, right foot bouncing up and down to the sounds emanating from her transistor radio. She "had soul" she had told him early on, with a casual irony Greer recognized as more than just wit. She used it as a shield, though he was starting to understand the funny girl wasn't always so tough.

Caroline was singing, belting out lyrics. Nothing was ever halfway with her. He ran up to her and gave her a quick kiss.

"I can't stay, I'm sorry," he said. "Another box came today, there's a clue."

"Oh, really? What'd you get?"

Greer took the letter out of his pocket and waved it around as an explanation. "I found something this time, I gotta go back."

"Already? Come on, baby. Sit down and stay awhile. Don't you like the Shirelles? She held her hand up to her mouth like a microphone and sang the song's title chorus right to him. "*Will you still love me tomorrow?*"

He smiled. Her voice didn't exactly lend itself to R&B, but it was just another quirk he found compelling. Greer remembered the first time she'd appeared at the river, looking for something different, wanting a surprise, she'd said. And she'd found it, Greer surprising himself, too, how much sway this breezy girl came to hold over him. How much he was willing to risk. He'd only been inside her car when parked in the woods, but he'd seen how she'd barrel along uneven country roads leading to their place, away from it, dust left in the wake, and always thought an actual drive with her might be more dangerous than someone seeing them together—not that they ever took that chance. They'd make love and he would open his hand wide to cup Caroline's breast, remarking on the contrast in skin tone, how lovely it was. "Write me a poem about it," she'd said. He did.

"Yeah, C, I will. So see you tomorrow."

Caroline stopped bobbing her head.

"Do you really have to leave?" she said. "We haven't even been anywhere yet."

Greer touched her hair. "Where do you want to go?"

"How about Hong Kong?" she said.

"Or Casablanca," he replied. It was their game—naming new places to escape to each day. They'd gone as far as getting their passports last week, "a real thing while we dream," each new blank space for a visa stamp a reverie in wait. Caroline was supposed to be starting college in the fall, "the older woman" she teased, but they'd begun wondering: what if they both just took off together? Was there a way?

"Ok, C, listen. I gotta see what else is in that box before my mama gets home. I know she'll hide it. Hey," he said noticing her look, "Why so sad? I'll see you tomorrow, ok? We'll go to Morocco. Or France."

"Promise?" For all her spunk Caroline could grow earnest, give him the simple expression of a girl who liked a boy. He couldn't describe how he swelled knowing he was that boy, against all odds, the one she lay down for.

"How could I stay away from magic?" he said. Their code word.

"Don't you forget it," she said. "Hey, let me see that note that's got you running away from me."

Greer handed it to her, though he was nervous to even let it go for one second. It seemed the most important document he'd ever received in his life.

"Wow," Caroline said. She kept staring at the note.

"Hey C, there aren't *that* many words on it," he said, starting to get a little restless.

She gave the note back to him. "This is a really big deal."

"I know," he said. "So let me get to it." He bent down and kissed her, then kissed her some more, before making himself stop. She was always hard to leave; like those cigarettes she'd turned him onto—addictive.

"See you soon, C."

As he walked away, he heard the music grow louder, Caroline having turned the volume up as high as it could go.

"Will you still love me tomorrow?"

*　　*　　*

Greer sighed relief that the house was still empty. The box was where he had left it, flaps still hanging open; for once the books left unattacked. He started taking them out, two, three at a time, and laying them on the floor. The few times before, he had hungrily scanned the titles, felt each book's weight, smelled the pages. This time he was looking for something else, though what exactly that would be, he wasn't sure.

In the bottom corner of the box sat another tiny box, gray and smooth. Greer picked it up delicately and opened it to find a thin silver necklace. He lifted the pendant between his fingers. He had never known his mother to wear adornments of any kind.

Greer turned the box over and found *Maier & Berkele* printed in flowing cursive script. Underneath it in smaller letters, *Atlanta, Georgia.*

Greer took the note out of his pocket again, an article—evidence?—now in each hand. He looked from one to the other, trying to make them fit.

"What are you doing?"

Greer jumped. Elizabeth's silent ways extended to how she moved. Greer always remarked that she seemed to float into rooms without making a sound. Even the creaking noise of the front door seemed to disappear under her hand.

"I'm the one who should be asking questions here, Mama. Who do you know in Atlanta? You know exactly who's behind these, don't you?" he said, getting up and motioning towards the box. "Why won't you tell me anything?"

Elizabeth stood before him, unwavering. Greer always marveled at this strange power his mother seemed to have, even while saying nothing. Later, he would be able to articulate that it is often silence that holds a stronger, more dangerous power than any other.

"Telling don't mean anything," she said finally.

"Why don't you let me be the judge of that? I have a right to know some things. We tiptoe around here, I'm not supposed to ask the simplest thing. You think I'm stupid? I can't handle the tiniest bit of truth?"

"I don't think that," his mother said, coming closer to him.

"Then what?" he said interrupting her, emboldened. "Why is everything such a mystery here? Who is J.T.?" he said, thrusting the paper at her.

Elizabeth gasped, swiping at the extended note. Greer drew it back, but not before she had torn a corner.

"You stop trying to snatch things away from me," he said. "You stop trying to keep things away that I should know. You don't want to tell me why there's someone sending me books, sending you jewelry, someone who knows I'm turning 16? I'll go to Atlanta myself. I'll go to this store," he said, holding out the jewelry box, above his mother's reach. "I'll go and ask them who, initials J.T., has recently bought this. I'll find out some things."

"You'll get yourself killed doing that, child," Elizabeth said, her eyes gleaming wild.

"I'm not a child anymore, Mama."

Elizabeth didn't say anything and he didn't wait for long. Greer rushed for the door, banging it open with his left shoulder, his hands still full of his evidence.

"Baby," she yelled after him.

Greer kept running, into an evening slowly descending into deep blue. He ran behind Wilson's General Store, and started down the path to Snake Creek. He wondered if Caroline might still be at their spot; he hadn't been gone that long. He wanted to be with her now, feel her slip her hand in his back pocket, whisper something daring in his ear. Being close to her was sometimes the only thing that kept him from flying apart.

He ran. When he reached the clearing his ribcage was sore and Caroline wasn't there. He walked down to the riverbed, kicking dirt up with each step. He was alone. He pitched his head backwards and yelled at the trees.

*   *   *

It was late when Greer returned home, though he had no watch and was in no hurry to get back. He had stayed by the river, his heart rate slowing, but his mind racing faster. The way out of town. How to get the address. Entry into the store, surely they wouldn't let him in. There were miles to cover. Borders. Race. Two initials and a feeling; was that enough? It was more than he'd ever had to go on before.

Greer opened the door and to his surprise found Elizabeth sitting in a chair facing the door. She nodded at him and told him to sit down.

Greer did, everything different today. He noticed that the box was gone from the living room and made a mental note to find it later.

"I won't go in for bearing more fatal mistakes," Elizabeth said.

Greer blanched at her cryptic language. "What does that mean, Mama?"

"I can't let you go into something that will only cause you trouble. I'm so glad you're here," she said, suddenly starting to weep. It wasn't the first time he had heard his mother cry—far from it—but it seemed the first time she had said anything like that to him. Listening to her muffled sounds drifting down the hallway late at night always made him feel he was partly responsible for her misery.

"I thought I might have lost you already, going to get yourself killed, following some crazy trail into the city. You know you can't do that."

"Well, Mama, I haven't left yet, but I'm going unless you tell me some things."

"I already lost someone. I watched it, I was there," Elizabeth said, almost as if in a trance, as if she hadn't heard him at all. "I couldn't do anything. I didn't." Greer nodded, holding his breath without realizing it.

"'This too shall pass.' That's what they say. There are some things that don't. They change, but they don't pass. I had a crazy grief after the drowning, after Major"—her breath caught as she said his name, and she stopped for a minute.

Greer lowered his eyes, giving his mother time to collect herself. He was vaguely aware of the note he still held, now damp from the moisture of his hand, softening from having been taken out and replaced, unfolded and re-creased so many times today. Elizabeth had said never to speak of the dead, and Greer had never pushed her, afraid that he would start her crying again. But the desire to ask never ceased. His father, the drowning, that mysterious night.

"I was trying to hold onto him," his mother said. "But then it started paining me to call you his family name, to remember my own mistakes."

Greer flinched as if stung. "I'm a mistake," he said.

"No, honey, that's not what I mean."

Greer looked at his mother, shadows falling across her face in the dimly lit room.

"I used to work on the other side," she said. "Still did after Major died. Mr. Thomas was there. I didn't stop him."

Greer sat immobile. The questions had been buried inside so long it almost hurt to voice them. *How did it happen, what's the other side like, tell me more about my father, who is Mr. Thomas.* "Stopped him from doing what?" he said, trying to hold his voice steady.

Elizabeth closed her eyes. "I didn't stop Mr. Thomas," she said again. "I didn't stop him till it kept on going and he told me he loved me. That wasn't love." She shook her head violently.

Greer looked down at his hands for a long time, the color Caroline called "pecan tan," and unfolded the note. The oblivious crickets chirped outside in the night. "I was born the wrong one," he said finally.

Elizabeth still had her eyes closed, her neck tense.

"So Mr. Thomas…J.T.?" he said.

"He doesn't have to be anything to you. He's not," she interrupted, her eyes flying open.

"He's my father," Greer said, trying to let this sink in.

"That means nothing."

"That means everything," Greer said. He was starting to tremble now. "That means everything and you deny me that."

"He's a white man who doesn't want anything to do with us."

"Then why does he send us these gifts? Maybe it's you. You don't love my father, but maybe I wanted a chance to."

Elizabeth sat back in her chair. Her voice took on the cold. "After everything I've just told you, you think I should have loved that man. You think I could have."

Greer's face grew hot. "No," he said. "No, Mama, I don't think that." He didn't know what to think. They sat silent for a few moments." I just…" he started, breaking through the thick air, "he's been sending these things to us."

"And in those boxes is our hush money." Elizabeth was talking in clipped sentences again.

"Hush money?"

"Don't you see?" Elizabeth turned her face towards the window. "There's a price for everything."

Greer felt a flush again, wondering what she could be remembering. All the questions he'd carried for so long now being replaced with new ones.

"Maybe he's trying to help," Greer said.

"Don't you know how things work around here?" she interrupted him, with an anger he'd never seen from her. "You go changing things now just to have your answers, there's no telling what there will be to pay."

Elizabeth wouldn't say any more. Greer sat there, searched her face, but it held nothing for him. He knew that look too well; she had tuned out the world. Nothing he could say would move her to speak further. He got up to find his books, wanting stories with simple resolution.

*   *   *

The house was larger than he had imagined, not that he had given much thought to dimensions. Other things, less concrete ones, had measure: the length of a man's absence, the distance between East Bannen and here, the width of the back road still hardly enough for two cars should they pass in the night. No, Greer knew the importance of detail—had absorbed it from the poems he would read to himself under faded sheets then experienced himself; how the earth could change rotation depending on the hue of the sky, how the smallest beauty mark on Caroline's back caused his heat to ignite.

But somehow he had no clear image of where J.T. might live—that name so recently gaining weight in his life. He had only the vague sense of what made a house a house if he pictured anything at all: foundation, bricks, eaves, roof. A place where a white man passed through hallways, hid behind walls, opened and closed doors. Windows.

Now, as a great green lawn with its blades of grass recently cut short stretched before him, it started sinking in. His father had lived here for all these years? Passed the potted flowerbeds each day. Had someone prune the shrubs in front. Thought nothing of those Greek columns, this imposing plantation house?

A lone woman wearing a long linen dress stood on the porch, a tall glass dripping sweat beads perched on the banister. She seemed to be looking out at a distance so far as to be almost invisible.

This he had not pictured. He'd barely had time to picture anything since his mother's revelation, everything moving so fast. She had finally conceded specifics, if only to save him from perilous false trails, and here he was, just a day later in what seemed an alien land. West Bannen. All he'd thought about was what to say to him. *Him.* He'd stayed up all night, arranged his text, assembled a speech strong enough that years later he could say he had stood up, even if just once. This scene, this reckoning, was to be between two men. That there would first be a woman gripping a railing had not occurred to him. He had no words for this woman.

Greer walked slowly towards the steps so as not to alarm her.

"Ma'am?" he said. His throat was dry.

The woman nodded curtly, but said nothing.

"I'm here to see Mr. Thomas." It was a statement, but his trembling voice lifted at the end into a question.

The woman didn't seem to hear him, or she made no acknowledgement.

He stood still as the silence lengthened. He was terrified to try again. But he was so close.

"Ma'am, I'm awfully sorry to intrude. May I speak to Mr. Thomas?"

The woman looked at him finally, though she didn't seem to quite see him. Nothing in her comportment changed as she gazed down; there was no stiffening or look of surprise, only a slight crease of suspicion on her forehead.

"I'm someone he knew a long time ago," he said. That wasn't quite true, but near to it. He didn't want to get into explanations too soon.

Her crease increased. He saw what she saw now: a young colored boy at the foot of some stairs saying he knew the district court judge of Leland County. If that didn't just beat all.

"I'm afraid the judge is indisposed at the moment. I'd be happy to pass along any message." She sounded as if she had speeches prepared, too. Perfected lines, well-trained talk.

"Please, ma'am," he said, "I've walked a long way. Please excuse my interruption, but I've come with a message meant only for him."

The woman stood still, her mouth growing tighter. He noticed her eyes and saw a look familiar to him, though seeing it on so foreign a face was odd. She looked weary. His mother carried that look, as well. Why was this a quality of so many women? To stand strong over men yet to ascend, at the same time so tired it seems they might fall down.

The woman stood still, focusing her eyes on her immeasurable distance. Greer waited, anxious. She could tell him no, to go, and because he was not here to make a scene with her—and for his own safety—he'd be obliged to obey.

A bee buzzed around him, but he tried to ignore it, afraid any sudden movement to swat it away might scare the woman. He heard the faint hum of a vacuum cleaner inside.

The woman finally turned and opened the screen door. She called into the interior—"Jefferson"—though Greer could not hear if any sound issued forth from the dark. She guided the door closed so it wouldn't clap like screen doors do, and went to sit in a wicker rocking chair. She didn't look at Greer any further.

A man appeared a few moments later, Greer having stood silent, waiting for what he suddenly felt unsure.

"What is it?" the white man said. Salt and pepper hair, a square, just face. Tall, almost eclipsing the doorway he stood in.

J.T.'s words hung in the air: *What is it?* To his wife or to him, Greer wondered to whom the question was directed. Were those to be the first words he received from his father?

"I would like to talk to you, sir."

"I don't have any business with you," J.T. said, looking down at him.

"I'm sorry, sir, but you do. You may not know it, but you do know me. Or you should."

The man looked over at his wife who stared at her clasped hands, then turned his gaze back to Greer.

"Please, sir," Greer tried. "There are some things I should say in private. I would not trouble the lady to hear it."

The man hesitated, then opened the door, holding it open, though not looking back. Greer mounted the steps and followed the man he had come to see. He looked straight ahead, but could feel the eyes of the woman watching him till he disappeared into the dark hallway. The ceiling inside was impossibly high.

*   *   *

There had been many smells. The coral honeysuckle that bloomed in mid-spring, the almost sickly sweet stench of Snake

Creek, the rare, greasy treat when there was chicken enough for frying. His mother's sadness almost had a scent, too. It was like a sachet of dried herbs left too long forgotten in an old shoebox at the bottom of a dusty closet, the odor so subtle you could hardly tell whether it was real or imagined. Sadness could have weight, it could have depth, but from as early as he could remember, Greer knew it also had a scent.

Sitting in Judge Thomas' study, the rich, deep smell of real leather surrounded him as he sat perched uncomfortably on an oversized chair, its back so tall it reached over his head. He wanted to stay straight up, alert. Leaning back into the chair's arch seemed undignified for the occasion, too casual, but there seemed no good way to hold himself. J.T. had his back to Greer, fixing himself a drink. That would be no way to begin—talking to a back.

Greer took in the floor-to-ceiling bookcases lining three of the walls to the study, leather-bound books filling each shelf. The books looked ordered, but used. From where he sat, he couldn't discern the titles of the books that comprised the Judge's collection. All those words bound with such care, preserved. Held secret, but beckoning to be opened. He closed his eyes, thinking of the musty books he'd received, the way his pulse would quicken. The way the smell of his mother's sadness grew stronger as she watched his delight. This man before him—it was he who had given him those prized gifts.

Greer clenched his jaw, an agitation rising, nothing having started in the right way. He had come here with what he thought was anger—righteous anger—but now he was feeling other things, too. He was distracted by the older woman on the porch carrying some affliction akin to his mother's, J.T.'s nonchalance, his own fear and doubt.

Greer waited for this man to make a drink so he could talk to him. He had had to think hard about whether it was worth risking—his mother had been able to provide for him on a promise to stay silent—but Greer was almost a man. He'd had enough of closed mouths, closed doors. He had things to say. Everything.

J.T. finally turned around with a glass in his hand, slowly swirling it. Greer saw that he already knew.

"Drink?" J.T. said. "You're old enough to drink now, I'm sure."

Greer never touched the stuff, never wanted to, though the few other boys his age were already beginning their ways with the brew. He couldn't stand the idea of some substance, some liquid, changing the way he carried himself. That men could succumb to some potion and lose control. If something were to happen, he wanted to know he alone were responsible. Unimpaired.

But now, stone cold sober, he felt his head swimming. He shook his head, unbalanced.

"There was no need for you to come," J.T. said.

Need? How could he talk about need? Greer studied J.T.'s face. Did he have his eyes? His jaw? Would his voice gain that deep timbre? "I *did* need to come, sir."

J.T. took a sip of his brandy and sat heavily into the chair across from Greer. "I know you and your mother have been well taken care of. I've seen to that."

Good to see you, son. That's what he'd wanted to hear. So much this man hadn't seen, Greer thought. "It's not just about that, sir."

"Just what do you think it is about? What are you doing showing up like this?"

"I have a right to. You kept us out of sight," Greer said, repeating what he'd practiced. "You took advantage of a woman who came into your house, looked after your family, then stashed her away."

"You don't know anything about that," J.T. said hotly.

Greer felt his cheeks flush. "Didn't you ever think I'd want to meet you, sir?" he asked more meekly. Didn't Mr. Thomas ever want to know him?

J.T. nodded, but Greer couldn't tell if he was agreeing or just shaking his head because he had nothing to say. "Elizabeth says you're smart. You devour every book from front to back."

"You talk to her?"

"Not really," J.T. said evasively. He flicked his eyes away to look at something behind Greer, then settled back on him.

Greer half turned, saw a clock on the wall.

"I have an appointment," J.T. said.

"I walked a long way to come here," Greer said, his anger returning. "You don't have ten minutes?"

"I had no warning you were coming," J.T. said. "I can't just drop everything."

"You have responsibilities, I'm sure," Greer said, his voice thick with irony.

"Careful." A deep vertical line appeared on J.T.'s forehead where before there had been none. He could look young or old depending on the expression on his face. "I'm surprised. You don't seem to know anything about crossing lines, where the lines even are. That's mighty dangerous. Someone should have taught you."

"And who should have done that?" Greer asked.

"Your mother let you talk back?"

"Leave her out of it."

J.T. stood up. Greer flinched, thinking he might be headed for him. Instead J.T. walked behind his desk, opened his briefcase. Shuffled some papers. At least, that's all he seemed to be doing to Greer. He was preparing to leave, wasn't he? Greer couldn't believe it.

"You owe me more than this," he said, standing up.

"Owe you?" J.T. slammed his briefcase shut. A framed photo on the desk fell from the force. "Look," he said, softening his voice, "things aren't so simple, I've done a lot more than someone else in my position would have done."

"And that's how you judge what's right?"

"You really are something."

"I'm your son," Greer said, the words that had been clawing behind his teeth the whole time. His whole life.

J.T. sighed. "You have a lot to learn," he said.

"That's why I'm here!" It pounded in him, all he wanted to learn, the years of wondering about his father, his father. What had he passed down to Greer? Would knowing this man explain why he'd always felt different? Could difference ever be a strength?

"It's time to go now. I'll see you to the back door."

"Like a dog, huh?"

J.T. shook his head. He righted the photo that had fallen on his desk, then picked up his briefcase. "My wife is sitting out there on the porch," he said, his lips now in a tight, thin line. "I'm going to show you out the back door. You're not going to look back, not at her, not at the house, and you're going to leave. I'm going to walk out the front door, give her a kiss if she'll even let me, and then go to the courthouse where I'm due. You can come back here tomorrow at five o'clock. Come in the same way as you leave now. We'll talk then."

J.T.'s voice vibrated with cool authority, but the words had stopped making their way into Greer's head halfway through.

"Did you hear me?" J.T. said when Greer didn't respond.

Greer glared at the photo J.T. had readjusted. At first Greer had merely glanced at it, a family portrait, his "real family" he had thought bitterly, but then something caught his eye and he had to look closer. J.T. in a suit and tie. The woman he'd met on the porch...

Greer walked forward slowly. He reached out and picked up the picture frame.

"What the hell are you doing?" J.T. said.

...Caroline in between.

Greer stared at the photo, then slowly back up at J.T. The *click-click-clicks* of the ceiling fan whirring softly overhead sounded spaced too far apart, everything in slow motion. The floor-to-ceiling bookcases seemed too close now, inching closer, the room claustrophobic and stale. A sharp taste of metal filled Greer's mouth. He shook his head. He could barely whisper it. *No.*

"What's wrong with you, boy?" J.T. said.

Greer took another look, then started backing up. He bumped into a chair, then a side table, then dropped the picture to the floor.

"The hell?" J.T. said.

Greer turned slowly. One foot, other foot, one foot, other foot. Then bolted for the front door.

"Boy!" his father called out, though Greer barely heard. Neither did he notice the colored woman, the help, cleaning in the den, nor see the woman on the porch, the wife, as she watched him hurry down the stairs.

He couldn't focus on any one thing. Nothing except his steps. One foot, two foot. One foot, two foot. He walked even quicker. One foot, two foot, one foot, two foot. Then he cut into a run. Faster and faster, he flew, running so hard only the rush of wind filled his ears. Legs, lungs, breath—he let his body take over. Legs, lungs, breath. All he knew was to keep running.

He sprinted into the trees lining the property and kept going, for how long he didn't know. He finally tripped over a branch and twisted his ankle. He lay there, sprawled on the ground, his breath rasping in and out.

Caroline had come across him reading Wordsworth in the woods one time, said her father adored that book, too. Greer called their first meeting their "prelude" though she said that was corny. He replayed the times they had stretched out along the river's edge, bodies intertwining. There was very little of the adolescent's awkwardness in their couplings; they seemed to know each other's bodies already.

Greer felt sick. He curled up into a ball, his back against the base of a tree. The sun moved lazily across the sky. The first dead leaves of fall speckled with its light. "Dads are overrated," she had whispered to him once, running her fingers gently through his hair.

Greer stayed there, set down in the Thomas' woods till dusk when the lightning bugs began to appear. He couldn't see any one thing clearly now, the world flashing between light and dark so fast.

CAROLINE THOMAS

(1961)

We shared the same bed, my brother and I. No one told me that, but it's a truth I know. Sense memory is strong, knowledge borne from the womb.

Most people enter this world struggling and singular, their faces pressed against pubic bone, the initial gasp for air the first in a long line of life's many lonely acts.

But I. I did not come into this world alone.

In our shared cradle, painted blue and mounted on sturdy oak rockers, Daniel and I cuddled together, twins, always by each other's side. A paper mobile of stars and moons and the stuff of sky floated above, just higher than tiny fists could reach. This was before language, before focused sight. We couldn't identify shapes—not of moving planets nor the two faces that repeatedly came close. Everything looked hazy, full of refracted light.

Mama. Dada. I spoke only the smallest of words at the time Daniel died. In a room where galaxies hung by hook and silver threads, he left the world quietly, gone in a bright night.

My parents thought I wouldn't remember; it happened before real speech. A toddler's visions—they would evaporate, disappear. Right?

But no one understands what it is to be that close. I felt the absence, even before I could fix names to facts. What to do with a heart that's hollow, haunted before you even start?

*   *   *

In our house, everything has its own specific place: Grandma's set of porcelain in the second kitchen cupboard, Mama's sheet music in the den's fold-top bench. We've always pretended life will run smooth if we put everything in compartments, tuck each and every thing away.

There's a little secret, though: we all know it doesn't work that way.

Daddy and Mama follow the script best they can—you could suffocate from all that's unspoken floating in the air. But I know the score; I've heard what's said behind closed doors. Why does no one realize? I'm smarter than I look.

Daddy was disappointed that I was the one left behind. No son to groom in his manner; no one to pass on the family name.

It should have been Daniel here.

It should have been me who died.

If that is so, I'm living on borrowed time. I can do what I please. Rules don't apply to me.

And what about those rules? How they burn me up. All the hypocrisy; everyone is blind.

This summer there's been a storm brewing, the Freedom Rides are rolling by. Every night on the news it becomes more and more clear; images seared on my mind. A bus firebombed in Anniston after leaving Atlanta. A mob of white people beating the unarmed. Which side is civilized? Who is really to blame?

And what about my Daddy? He's one to speak of right or wrong, no matter that he's a judge. He had another woman, a colored one, too. People saying one thing, then doing something else.

The fine upstanding families of Bannen. It's all a farce. My parents don't look at each other; they don't care for me.

Test the limits; bend, I don't break.

Everyone's the same here. The stupid boys I go to high school with. The 'good girls' we know are thinking something else. I want something different. I go to see with my own eyes before I decide.

Cross a line and what happens? Who did I meet, but Greer? A gentle boy, a poet even, who saved me from the waves. On the other side, I found truth. On the other side is grace.

I don't care what anybody has to say. Meeting Greer was my destiny. He is my fate. We've created our own mythic past. I am once again united with my other half. Born in Snake Creek, the world began with us. Covered in river like fluid from the amniotic sac.

I love him, our strong and strange connection. I'll go with him to the ends of the earth if need be. It's time to get away. We will be free.

EXILE

(1961)

From the Thomas' house, Greer snuck through the forest like some nocturnal animal. And that's what he was, wasn't it? Nothing more than a beast. His mind held darkness, the black night equal to his primordial thoughts. Only, not just his thoughts had turned on him. His whole body rebelled.

Caroline and I share blood?

For the first time in his life, Greer understood how a person might simply give up.

The photograph, he couldn't stop picturing it over and over again. And remembering, details, all those sweet little nothings they'd whispered to each other now took on sinister meanings. Why? Why did this happen?

Greer had to stop at one point and lean against the solid trunk of an oak tree. *"Will you still love me tomorrow?"* Was it really only yesterday Caroline had sung that song to him? The lighthearted joke. The serious answer. Less than an hour with a father he'd sought for sixteen years and instead this the revelation: love as abomination.

Greer didn't know what time it was when he could finally start moving again or if Caroline would still be waiting for him at their spot.

But she was. Of course she was. He stayed back; she hadn't seen him yet. How in the world would he face her? What was he going to say? He watched her from behind a tree. She pulled at the grass, checked her watch, frowned. Then her face cleared again. Hopeful. Shining. Expectant.

Greer clasped his hands over his mouth. It was physical, this pain. She was watery, as he'd first seen her, but this time because of the tears in his eyes. He watched her there, shimmering, innocent, beautiful.

He couldn't do it. He could not. He receded back into the trees, careful not to make any noise. When he was far enough away he released the cries. But at the center, the essence remained silent. The heart breaks, but it makes no sound.

*   *   *

At this time of night, Greer was the only soul walking down Main Street. Bannen's quiet, as usual, filled the air. The town always seemed capable of sleeping while all the world burned.

A small light shone through the front window of his house. His mother had surely stayed up for him. She surely knew where he had gone. Greer's anger rose.

He turned the key slowly in the door, tried to keep the deadbolt from making its sudden metallic snap. Elizabeth was the only person in Bannen to have such a lock.

His mother sat slumped upright in that rickety rocking chair in the living room, her head fallen to one side. Greer stopped and looked at her, tried to imagine for just a moment her face pressed against Mr. Thomas', the picture of who had made him finally complete.

But the other picture flashed brighter.

It took all he had to quell a strong urge. *See what you've done*, he wanted to scream at her. *Look at what's happened*, as he shook her violently in the chair.

Instead he went to his room. He couldn't have her awake. He saw the box pushed towards the far corner as if it were hiding. This box that had just arrived, opened with excitement, had unleashed so much. Nothing hidden anymore.

Greer looked around his room. Could a life fit in a box? he wondered. He had few possessions: a lamp, notebook paper, pencils with worn erasers. The books Judge Thomas had sent from his vast library lined up on the shelf. He remembered the smell of leather, the brief glimpse of that floor-to-ceiling library today. Was it only just today?

Greer grabbed his small duffel bag from under his desk—an old thing too small for the man he'd become—and began emptying his drawers. What did one need really? Three T-shirts, two pairs of pants, underwear and socks for a week. The shoes on his feet.

He scanned the titles of the books against the wall. This would take the most time, choosing which slim volumes could carry him through what lay ahead. He fingered a few of his favorites, but soon picked up this new book that had remained untouched. The events of the previous few days had left no time for browsing. It was a gamble to choose something he'd never read, but he threw it in his knapsack. *Self Reliance*. That's what he'd be needing now, wasn't it?

Greer zipped the bag whose strap seemed to hang by only a thread. Then he thought of something. He walked over to the box and peered inside. The small gray jewelry case containing the delicate silver necklace destined for his mother still sat at the bottom. Greer had never taken anything from anybody. But he thought now of all that had been taken from him.

He picked up the jewelry box and put it in his bag. He knew the necklace must be valuable and the only thing of worth he might sell.

The matter of possessions now in order, he turned to the rest—everything. Caroline. Greer started trembling. He closed his eyes, saw her fresh face, pink day dress, felt her arms around his neck. Hot, angry tears streamed down his face.

He sat down at his desk and tried writing a letter, but each attempt ended up a crumpled sheet on the floor. He couldn't even hold his hand steady, much less know what to say.

He got up again and paced the room. Then remembered. He lifted his mattress and found the passport he'd put there just last week. All of the places they'd dreamed of going! Greer went back to the desk and wrote the most basic truth he knew: *C, I'm sorry. I just have to go. G*

Greer wondered how to get the note to her. Did he trust the mail? A letter from East Bannen to West. In that big white house over there, would someone else open it first?

By the time Greer left with his meager belongings he had made a decision. An unsealed envelope marked *Caroline Thomas* lay on the kitchen table for his mother to find. She would do what she would with it. Deliver it? Burn it? Curse? Weep? At least she would know why he had left. She would understand what she had wrought.

When Greer was a little ways out of town, he stopped to set fire to the rest of the letters he had started and failed to write. Bright flames leapt in the night, a dance that seemed too joyous for the surrounding darkness. Greer was sure Bannen had seen the last of his flames.

*   *   *

For such a large ship, the SS Spirit tackled the sea not like a sturdy ocean liner, but as a tugboat at the water's mercy, each new wave a monstrous mountain to climb. That's how it felt to Greer, at least, who had been sick every day for the past week. This seemed to be the emerging lesson of late—forces in motion can make you retch.

The journey across the Atlantic was clocked at ten days. Affected almost immediately by a strange, queasy feeling in his gut, he had set himself a stripped-down schedule: a strict rotation of curling up in the fetal position down in the ship's pit, and standing outside on the prow where the salt air sometimes offered a moment's reprieve.

That fellow Louis hadn't mentioned anything about this nauseating sway. When Greer had hawked his mother's necklace in the pawn shop, the man had offered up the suggestion—cheap tickets on freighters take you far, far away. They even took colored boys. Louis saw enough people pass through to recognize the different faces of desperation. Some only needed cash. Some, escape.

Today, the seventh day on board, the waters ran rough, an impending storm on the horizon. Greer leaned against the railing on the navigation bridge. He waited for the rain, hoping the fresh water might revive him. There seemed something fitting about the nausea, though, this passage like a surreal continuation, being carried from one sick dream to the next. Maybe he would feel like this forever.

There were no other passengers around; it was mostly crew on the ship, anyway. As it was, Greer tried to stay out of sight. He was hard not to notice, though—a young colored boy, so obviously alone. Reaching out for something, anything, to hold onto.

The storm surged into being with violence. How quickly these things came. Rain fell in tight sheets. The pounding water beat down on Greer, the elements pushing him this way and that. The ship rocked from side to side.

When the wind whipped him hard into the railing, he was brought momentarily to the edge, off-balance. Only a small calculation kept him from falling over. The thought flickered past: why not? Maybe the dark water was where he belonged. Why should he cling to life?

Yet he did.

You saved my life. Now we're bound forever.

Little could be seen in the downpour except loud streaks of lightning over the water, their jagged lines terrifying the open sky. Greer vomited again, some of the foul juice coming back to hit him in his face, the rain washing it away. Was it possible to expel everything from your insides? Could one purge all that was unholy?

The storm's sound and fury, his own delirium and sickness conspired with the blinding flashes of light. As Greer lost both up and down, inside and out, his mind's eye conjured up an image of a strange state he had only witnessed in a veiled fashion—overheard shouts from the chapel, glimpses of writhing bodies through warped glass.

'Pleading the blood' is what the church folks called it—the thrashing and threshing of a soul passing through fire. But why would he think of it now? Those folks reached towards deliverance. That trance ended in salvation, a fainting spirit brought through.

What if you were never brought through? Greer wondered, the storm raging around him. What if, for all the pleading, you remained in the fire?

Or in the drowning rain?

*   *   *

When Greer woke up, he was in a clean, dry place, a crisp, white linen across him, the sheet tucked into a squeaky cot. He saw a white man in what seemed to be sailor's clothes busy with something in the corner, what he couldn't tell.

Greer coughed. His throat felt raw.

"Ah, coming to," the man said, turning toward him. "We're almost there."

"Where?" Greer asked, looking around. "Where am I?"

"You were dehydrated, had a fever. Lucky we found you when we did. What were you doing out there, mate?"

Greer was still groggy, the details hazy. Hard rain and bright lights—that's all he could remember.

"Here," the man said, handing him some water, "drink up."

Greer tried to sit up a little and spilled some of the liquid as he brought it to his mouth.

"Easy does it," the man said.

"Weak," Greer croaked.

"Someone on the other side for you, kid? Who do you know in France?"

"France?" Greer said, confused. "I don't know anyone anywhere."

The man studied Greer's face. "What brings you this way? You remember where you're going?"

"I'm gone," Greer said, images of his disorienting night starting to seep back in.

"What's that?"

"It sends me. I'm gone." These were things the church folks said when they pleaded the blood. Greer felt gone, but not in the way they must mean it. Just gone.

"Maybe you better get some more rest there, kid. You're still a bit out of it, eh?"

Greer put the water down beside the cot and laid his head back down. He didn't care about anything. He closed his eyes and was out again.

*   *   *

By the time the ship arrived in Le Havre, he had recovered. Physically, at least. "You got your sea legs," Rick, the man who had tended to him said. "Just in time." Greer didn't know about his legs—it seemed his gut was the problem. But now the rocking didn't seem to bother him at all, as if the fire of his sickness had cleansed him somehow, purged the nausea straight out of him. He was sorry he had only the last day to experience the calm of the ocean.

The harbor was in sight. They didn't seem to be doing anything, though—just waiting. The crew had completed all the preliminary preparations, so there wasn't much left to do until they docked.

Rick spotted him and came over.

"Small locks in Le Havre. Got to be patient. It's always congested here."

Greer looked out at the port: pulleys, machines, iron, steel. This was what he'd be walking into.

"You gonna be all right, kid?" Rick said.

"I just got on the first ship that would take me," Greer said.

"Yeah," Rick said. "That's the way."

They stood there for a moment, Greer looking at the industrial landscape. Everything seemed cold and mechanical all of a sudden, the sound of iron against iron. The smell of oil hung heavy in the air.

"Maybe you should head down to Paris," Rick said. "There's not much for you here. Plenty of pretty boys like you have made it down there."

What did he mean, "pretty boys like him?"

Rick lit a cigarette. Greer looked at it, almost longingly. "What, you want one?" Rick asked.

"I would, thank you."

Rick, raising his eyebrows in surprise, handed one over. "Tougher than you look, kid."

"Yeah, well," he said. "Don't know if looks are to be believed."

Rick nodded. He had a nice face, rough hands. Stubble. Greer wondered how long he'd been out on the sea.

"What exactly do you do on the ship?" Greer asked.

"Second mate, mate," Rick said, smiling. "Make sure everything's in order."

"And you just live on this ship?"

"Nine months out of the year," he said. "Suits me just fine."

Greer took a drag on his cigarette. "Doesn't seem like it'd be too bad."

"No, it's not bad at all. Get to see a lot of places, though after a while every port starts to look the same."

"I've never seen anything like it," Greer said.

"You get used to it. Guys miss their family, though."

Family. The word stung.

"I don't have to worry about that," Greer said.

"Oh?" Rick said, taking a long drag on his cigarette. He ashed in the sea, blew a long exhale. "I signed up young, too, kid."

When the ship finally pulled in, everything was abuzz again on board. The crew started unloading, some of those large cranes and pulleys Greer had been eyeing coming close for the cargo.

Rick had scribbled the name of a hotel in Le Havre, one in Paris. "Just in case," he said.

Greer walked off the ship onto a different shore.

Part Two:
Present and Future

SEVEN

(1977)

"There's no difference!" Ceiley said, delighted.

"I swear, there is. *Minnyim. Me nyim.* See?" Greer said. "*Minnyim, me nyim.*"

Ceiley crossed an arm across her stomach. "Ow, stop," she said dissolving into a laughing fit.

They sat on Greer's porch with Ceiley's book bag open nearby. School had just started back up after the eventful summer break, though the late August sun didn't do much to mark the occasion. There was still the regular heat; it was simply the daily rhythm that had changed. Rather than their leisurely afternoon talks, Ceiley now visited after class. Today, Ceiley had come for help with her English homework, so Greer's "book learning" as her mama called it could be put to some use, but they'd gotten talking about other languages instead.

"OK, so which one means 'I know?'" Ceiley asked.

"*Me nyim,*" Greer said.

"And 'I don't know.'"

"*Minnyim.*"

"That's crazy. And you understand that?"

Greer smiled as he nodded. It was always a highlight to hit upon something that tickled Ceiley so much. He searched for these tidbits. Plus, her laugh was hilarious. Who couldn't use the shot of joy?

"I know I don't know," Ceiley said. "I don't know I know."

"You got it," he said.

"That's a good one."

"I didn't even tell you the best part," Greer said. "'I'm pregnant.' It sounds the same, too."

"You're pregnant!" she exclaimed. "No way. Can't be true."

"I'm telling you. Akan's a tonal language. Three different tones right there."

"I don't know I know I'm pregnant," Ceiley doubled over again. "*Minnyimminnyimminnyim.* Mama could use that one."

"Now don't go hurting her feelings."

Ceiley shook her head, still laughing. "No, no. I mean, I know."

"Ok, so how did we even get on this anyway?" Greer said, reaching for her book. "You have to finish your essay."

"I don't get this poem, that's how we got here. I know I don't know what it's about. How am I supposed to analyze it?" she said. "And what the heck is a seraph?"

"An angel," Greer said. "The top kind of angel."

"And covet?"

"It means to want something, but really, really badly. Sometimes in a bad way."

"So why can't he just say that?"

"It's poetry, right? This is how we create *our* tones. Listen, read the lines:

I was a child and *she* was a child
In this kingdom by the sea,
But we loved with a love that was more than love—
I and my Annabel Lee—"

"That's a lot of love."

"Yeah, exactly. It draws our attention to the main theme. And see how it creates a beat?" He tapped his hand against his leg as he read it again. "Poe did that on purpose."

Ceiley studied the text. "Ok, but basically this whole thing is creepy. I mean you told me he's sleeping in her tomb."

"Yeah. But it makes you feel something."

"Um, yeah. Creeped out."

"Well good if it gets to you. Every writer wants you to feel something. Isn't it amazing that just those words alone can give you goosebumps?"

"I guess. I liked listening when you were speaking French better. I don't have to understand the words to know it sounds pretty."

"That's what you're supposed to write about. The *sounds* in the poem, not just what it's about. So read it aloud. See what you hear. The rhythm. The repetition. The *tone*," he said dropping his voice in a faux dramatic fashion.

Ceiley laughed. "Ok, thanks, Greer. Makes more sense now." She stood up and grabbed her backpack and her book. "Dinner time, you know."

"Oh, I know, *Mademoiselle*," he said. "*Me nyim*."

"You're silly," she said, before crossing the street to her house.

He should get started on dinner, too, but he stayed where he was. The sun was just starting to set. The sky wore deep blues slashed by pink. If he sat and watched it long enough, it would keep changing before his eyes.

What he knew, and what he didn't know. It was something he ruminated on quite a bit. Not just a trick of language; it had taken him years in Ghana before he heard the difference in those tones, too. Gloria had helped him hear a lot of new things. But the deeper knowledge, the kind understood at a level even beyond words—that was different. The same experience could be changed radically by what you did and did not know. Wasn't that the heart of his young life's tragedy?

"'It was many and many a year ago/In a kingdom by the sea.'" God, it had been a long time since he'd read that poem. The obsession. The loss.

Greer stood up and went inside to make something for him and Elizabeth to eat. Standing over the stove, waiting for the cooking oil to heat, he knew what he had to do. What he'd known as soon as he'd come back. He hoped he wasn't as far gone as Edgar Allan Poe, but he'd been in town long enough: it was time to find Caroline.

EIGHT

(1977)

B ack then, the road to West Bannen began as a dirt path, just like every other street that started in the East. Now it was paved the whole way, both sides connected via asphalt, tar mirages wavering in the air. Spots in the distance appeared to gather invisible force, shudder, then disappear at the approach.

Greer didn't need to look at a map to remember the route to the Thomas', though it had been years since he'd been there and it wasn't all that close by. Some things he remembered with perfect clarity, even if he wished he didn't.

The humidity hung heavy; his legs felt leaden, but he let compulsion carry him. This journey was necessary. What had he been doing all this time, anyway, except circling around old wounds? When had he ever *not* been thinking about what had happened here?

The last time he had set off to this side of town, he had thought all of his questions would be answered, his ever-present yearning finally fulfilled. Instead, bright new torments were born. The demands on his soul afterwards didn't even begin to have a name.

This time, Greer tried to empty himself, expect nothing. Tried hard not to want. What *could* he want? In the best of scenarios, what could he hope for now?

Greer focused on the sound of his footsteps. He had planned to take his bike at first, but he decided he needed the simple reminder of his feet landing on solid ground today. It sometimes amazed him to think of it—how your whole world could turn upside down and yet nothing on the outside shifted.

A dense thicket of pine trees still lined the Thomas' property, though sections had been cleared to make room for smaller houses. He kept walking past the trees, trying not to remember the aftermath. His stomach turned anyway.

When he reached the house, he stood in front, taking stock. His palms were sweaty. He noticed the peeling paint on the banister, holes in an ill-fitting window screen. The house was still imposing, but it seemed tired and used, too. The five steps up to the porch struck him as high, steep. He wasn't sure if he was ready. But when would he be?

He lifted his heavy feet and climbed the stairs. Left foot, right foot. Breaking the movement down to simple commands. At the door he saw both a knocker and a bell. He didn't know which to reach for. Finally he opened the screen door and held the heavy brass knocker in his hand before rapping three times quickly so he couldn't change his mind. He shut the screen door again and waited.

He waited a long time. No one came. His heart, in his throat, slowly started descending.

He opened the door again and banged as loud as he could this time.

Finally, the door opened, a curious black face looking at him through the mesh. "Hardly even heard you from back there. Didn't you see the bell?"

"Afternoon," Greer said. "Is…" He paused, realizing he didn't even know who to ask for first. "Is Caroline Thomas in? Mr. Thomas?"

The woman looked confused. "Thomas?"

"Any of the Thomases? The Judge? His daughter?"

"Sorry, son, there are no Thomases here," the woman said. "Burnwoods."

"Burnwoods?"

"That's right. Mr. and Mrs. Alton Burnwoods. Didn't you see the letterbox out front?"

"No, ma'am, I didn't." Greer stood there, not sure what to do next. "Do you know the people who lived here before?"

"I sure don't," said the woman. "Been with the Burnwoods for years."

Greer tried to run through his options. Why should he be surprised? How often had he moved in the last decade and a half?

"I don't know what to tell you," she said, as Greer made no motion to leave.

"When did you say they moved in here?"

"Oh, let's see," she said, counting. "Coming up on fifteen years now. 1962, it was."

"So right after," Greer said.

"Sorry, son? Right after what?"

"I'm sorry. I just, well, I need to find the people who lived here before."

"Mm-hmm," the woman said. "I see."

"It's important."

They stood looking at each other through the mesh. "Well, looks to be, now don't it?" she said.

"Yes, ma'am."

The woman gripped a broom in her hands—he just now noticed. She must have been cleaning when he knocked. An image flickered through his mind, his mother cleaning this same house, too. Strange, he had so rarely pictured that.

"I sure don't like to trouble them," the woman said, "but I'll go in and see if someone will talk to you. Maybe Thomas rings a bell."

"Thank you kindly, ma'am. I appreciate it."

The woman shuffled off again.

Greer walked to the edge of the porch, put his hands on the railing. He let his head and shoulders slump over a little. Where were they? Not here. Not anymore. Disappointment and relief started creeping in.

"Can I help you?" a man's voice came from behind him.

Greer quickly straightened up and turned around. He half expected to see Mr. Thomas, the way you hope against hope, but of course it wasn't him. "Yes, sir, thank you. I'm trying to find out what happened to the family that lived here before. The Thomases?"

"That's what Cornelia said."

For a second, Greer wasn't sure who Cornelia was, then realized it must be the woman he had just spoken to. "Yes, sir. I would appreciate it if you had any information. I didn't know they'd left."

"Woo-ee, you've been gone awhile then," the man said. "They haven't been here for years."

"Right. I knew them when I was younger."

"You knew them, huh?" The man's expression grew more skeptical. "Well, property sales are a matter of public record. You can just go on over to the county tax office and look up that information if you need. I don't go around telling other people's business like that."

"I respect that, sir. I do."

"Anyhow, I don't know what happened to them after we bought this place from them. Seemed like good people. Torn up."

Greer felt a pain in his chest. "I imagine so."

"Shame about their girl. Good family."

"Caroline?" he said, his throat going dry.

"That was her name, I believe," the man said. "Guess maybe you do know them."

"Yes, sir, I do."

"Yeah, well, they sold the house to us. Said it was too big for just the two of them. Funny because me and Shelley never even had kids, but the house doesn't feel too big."

"A lot happened," Greer said, his mind racing. What about Caroline?

"A lot always does."

"What did you say happened to Caroline?"

The man's eyes narrowed. "Didn't say," he said.

"Ok," Greer said.

The man just looked at him, still looking him over. Finally he said, "Must have been that she ran off. They didn't really go into it. Guess they couldn't stand living in the house after that."

"Ran away?" Greer said. Were their paths always to mirror one another's? "No one knows where?"

"Well if they knew that, I guess they would have found her. Now listen, I think that's about all I know."

Greer could feel the man's impatience growing. He just had to ask one last question. "And Mr. Thomas? Is he still in town?"

The man looked at him hard. "Well, I reckon it'd be easier to track down a Judge than a run-away, don't you?" he said.

"Thank you, sir. Sorry to have troubled you."

Greer turned to go. He walked down the steps almost as heavy as when he walked up them.

"Aw, hell," the man called out to him. Greer turned back. "Might as well tell you. They're sure as hell not in West Bannen. We'd know about it if any of them were still here. Small town."

"Sure is," Greer said.

"What was your name again?" the man asked.

What was it to him?

"What are you looking for, boy?"

The question hung clear in the air. He was far enough away now that there was no need to respond. Greer stumbled back the way he'd come, the only answer a pregnant silence.

NINE

(1977)

The Leland County tax office stood out for its large revival bell and clock tower, a brick courthouse trimmed in granite. It was more regal than he'd imagined, though he shouldn't have doubted otherwise considering all official business took place here.

Greer had never been to Grant, the county seat. He'd breezed through scores of back roads and towns on his way to Savannah's port years ago, but he hadn't paid attention to names. He hadn't paid attention to much then, only to getting out.

Grant certainly had more points of interest than Bannen, but he wasn't there for sightseeing. He didn't know what good it'd do to look up the records for the Thomas' old house. Wouldn't it just say who bought it? He already knew the answer to that now. But he had to keep digging.

Greer hadn't articulated, not to anyone, not even to himself, what he hoped to find. What would he even say to Caroline or his father if he did manage to track them down? All he knew was that he'd traveled the globe and they'd come along with him. Caroline especially seemed to pulse through his very veins.

Today he'd taken his bike. After locking it up out front, he entered the building. The woman at the information desk pointed him to the room containing property records—first floor, last door on the left. Staffed by two older white women, the room was stuffy and hot. A fan propped in the window whirred on medium speed. They were the only three people there.

One of the women sat fanning herself in a fold-out chair. She looked bored as all get out. The other woman, "Belle" emblazoned on her blouse, seemed interested in helping Greer. The office wasn't exactly a high-traffic area. What else was she going to do?

"Amazing how far back these records go, isn't it?" she said, as she combed through the files.

"Yes, ma'am," Greer said. "It's a good service you run here."

"Oh yes," she said. "What's a town without its history?"

A place without pain? Greer thought. But he continued making pleasantries.

"Here we go," she said, handing him a file for 57 Whittier Place, West Bannen, Georgia. "You should find what you need in there."

"Thank you," he said, and took the folder to the table in the center of the room. He flipped the pages over one by one and soon found a copy of the deed.

"May 17, 1962," he muttered.

"What's that?" the woman said.

"Oh sorry," he said, a little startled. He hadn't realized he had spoken aloud, or that Belle had followed him over and was peeking over his shoulder.

"Oh yes, Jefferson Thomas, we remember them all right."

"Oh yeah?" Greer said, regarding Belle with new interest.

"Wasn't that a scandal," she said. "Remember that,

Bernice?" she called out to the other woman. "Weren't those Thomases a scandal?"

Bernice fanned herself. "Sure was," she said, still sounding bored.

"What happened?" Greer said. "I didn't hear much about it."

"Well, I guess not. Suppose you're from *East* Bannen," she said, and looked for a moment like she might shut her mouth on her gossip.

Greer felt his cheeks grow hot, but he gave her his warmest smile. The thing about his coloring, he was obviously of mixed race, but he looked different enough that he could often make white folks comfortable enough if he tried to. He wasn't *that* black. He knew that's what they thought.

"Well darn it if he didn't lose his appointment a cause of his wife," she said.

"A political appointment."

"Uh-huh. He didn't just want to be a county judge, you know."

"He wanted more power," he said.

"Oh shoot, men always want more."

Greer heard Bernice grunt in agreement.

"Well, Susan went and left him, now didn't she?" Belle said. "No way he was getting a seat after that."

"His wife?" he said.

"Of course. Left his name behind, too."

"She sure did," the other woman chimed in.

"Plain old Susan Newman," Belle said. "That might have been a first around here."

"Oh no, it wasn't. Don't you remember Alma Macon? Left old Charlie in the dust and took on that raggedy old name of hers?"

"Oh yeah, wasn't that the darnedest thing? Who'd go back to being a Boatwright? You'd think she'd a thanked her lucky stars to have escaped that wretched family."

Greer jotted *Susan Newman* on a notepad while the two women continued talking. They were on a tear.

Newman. He underlined the name, then made two separate lines underneath that. New man.

"Excuse me, ma'am?" he said, trying gently to interrupt the two women now busy with their gabbing, "do you know how I'd find either Mr. Thomas or Mrs…Mrs. Newman?"

"Oh, now, let's see," Belle said.

Bernice pulled her face tight and went back to fanning herself.

"Can't say I've seen hide or tail of any of the Thomas folk in a long while," Belle said. "You, Bernice?"

"Uh-uh," Bernice grunted.

"Susan went on and set herself up in Hickory for a little while, I heard. Don't know what became of the Judge after he left town."

"Hickory's just a few towns over, right?" Greer said, jotting that down, as well.

"Oh yeah, just a stretch on down Tupelo, past the old turpentine still."

"They had a daughter, too," Greer said, a lump in his throat again.

"Ran off, I think. With that feller? Who was it, Bernice?"

"Well damn, Belle, I can't keep track of everyone's business, can I? We're not the ancient history department."

Belle turned back to Greer. "Maybe that's what started all the hoopla, who knows?"

Greer felt sick again—what *feller?*—but he stacked all of the papers in a neat pile and thanked them kindly. "It's been a pleasure."

Now it was Belle who blushed. "Just doing our job," she said.

"You do it well," he said.

*   *   *

It took him over an hour to bike to Hickory from Grant. He had an address of the only Susan Newman in that town and any of a number of surrounding ones, too. He'd looked up from the pages of the phonebook, surprised by how easy it was. No unlisted number. Not a long list of people with the same name. Just one. Could it really be her? The wife—*ex*-wife—of Judge Thomas? Caroline's mother?

On his notepad, next to *Susan Newman*, he'd drawn an arrow, then *Caroline Newman?* with a big question mark.

With the day starting to wane, he'd decided to go directly there. Why stop? He didn't know when he'd get another chance to be away for so long; Elizabeth needed more and more help. Esse had offered to look in on her today, but he couldn't rely on always finding a willing volunteer.

It turned out Susan Newman lived in a small house not far from the mill. Two units sat side by side with a shared porch, shingles that needed redoing running across the roof. The house on the left had a brown welcome mat laid down with ceramic animal figurines lined up beside it. The house on the right was bare, as if it didn't want to draw attention to itself. Susan Newman lived there.

Greer left his bike leaning against a cedar tree out front. He stepped up, just one step, and stood in front of the white door with no sign. He drew a deep breath and rang the bell this time.

A minute passed. He heard someone come to the other side of the door. "Who is it?" a woman's voice asked.

"I'm looking for Susan Newman," Greer said.

"And I asked who's calling."

"Mrs. Thomas?" he said.

At that, the voice fell silent.

Greer waited a few seconds, then continued. "I'm sorry to trouble you, ma'am. If I could just talk to you a few minutes." After another long pause, the door slowly opened halfway. The woman peered out at Greer.

"Good evening, ma'am," Greer said, taking a step back. It was always best to show you didn't mean to storm in.

"What do you want?" Susan asked. "Who are you?"

"I don't know how to say this, Mrs...Newman?" he said, still unsure of the name. He'd been carrying "Thomas" around with him for so long.

The door opened wider. She sized him up. "Wait a minute," she said, dragging out the words, "I know who you are."

"Yes, ma'am." He tried not to look too closely at her.

"I know who you are," she said again. "What the hell are you doing here?"

Greer was surprised by the profanity. "I'm not here to cause any trouble."

"Trouble? You want to talk about trouble?" she said.

"Ma'am, I really mean no harm."

"I don't even know what you're doing on my porch," she said.

"I didn't mean any harm."

"Can't keep away, can you?" she said. "I can't believe it."

"I won't keep you long," he said.

"It's never going to end, is it?" she said, shaking her head from side to side. "Your family has brought nothing but damnation."

Greer's blood went cold. He nodded gravely. "I really didn't want to have to involve you, ma'am."

"And here you are again."

"I know you're not a part of this."

"Not a part? You tear my family asunder and I'm not a part?"

"I'm sorry," he said. "This isn't going the way I meant it to."

She made one loud, punctuated sound. A laugh, if it weren't so bitter. "How did you mean for this to go?"

"Caroline," he said, uselessly. "I don't know."

Susan let out a big sigh and slumped against the doorway. She wasn't even looking at Greer anymore. "Everything just collapses," she said.

"If I could set things right," he said.

"The things I tried to forgive."

"I didn't know," he said.

"She told me you saved her life. She begged me to understand," she said, her whole body beginning to tense again. She straightened up all of a sudden and looked him square in the eye. "Her life? You ruined it," she said and spat at him. She slammed the door shut.

Greer stood facing the door, stunned. He reached his right hand up to his cheek, felt the warm saliva in his fingers. He took a handkerchief from his pocket and wiped the rest away, put the soiled cloth into his pocket again. Backing away slowly, he missed the step off the porch and fell down.

He could feel it, the shakes starting to come on all over. He pulled himself up with the banister's help, then sat down heavily on the porch; his legs didn't seem able to hold him. If he could have just laid down and never gotten up again he would have.

There was none of that, though. The door flung open again and Susan charged over to him. "You get away from here," she said, kicking him. He stumbled to his feet. "You get away and don't you ever come back."

Greer put his hands up to shield himself and backed away. She was slapping at any piece of him she could, working herself into a frenzy.

"You want to talk about Caroline? How could you?"

"I'm sorry," he was saying in between blows. She was half screaming, half crying.

"We took care of it. How dare you? No baby anymore."

Greer dropped his arms in surprise. "Baby?" he said, a split second before Susan knocked him hard in his face, now unprotected.

"Mrs. Newman? You ok?" he heard a man call out. People were coming out onto their porches now. No one from the house next door, but others.

"Nigger's beating up on Mrs. Newman," someone said. Then more voices.

For an instant Greer faltered—what had Mrs. Thomas said?—but he saw people starting towards him. He turned and grabbed his bike resting against the tree. He could barely get it upright with Susan hitting him.

"Hang on there, boy." Men were running now. He had to push Mrs. Thomas away to get on his bike.

"You killed everything, you killed everything," she was screaming.

His legs were so wobbly he didn't know if they'd work, but fear put his feet on the pedals. He took off as fast as he could. He heard loud voices behind him, a car starting up its engine. He looked back once, the sight too scary that he looked back ahead and peddled even faster. He dashed off the main road, onto a gravel side street leading to a patch of woods. The car was right on his heels. Light had left the sky.

On the edge of the woods, he went off-road, plunged straight into a thicket, thick as cobwebs. Brambles and branches scratched at his face, his whole body. He couldn't see anything, but he kept on, ignoring the onslaught of thorns that dug into his skin. He bumped up and down, the ground so uneven it was hard to stay on his seat.

No one else made it in that far, though. The car couldn't penetrate the thicket, the people on foot too slow to catch up with him. As he pushed further into the woods, all he heard were branches knocking against each other, wheels turning, and his own voice, though he didn't recognize it at first, yelling into the darkness.

*   *   *

When he returned home late that night, Esse and Ceiley were dozing off on Elizabeth's couch. They quickly woke up, though.

"Good gracious!" Esse said, getting up when she saw him.

Greer didn't say anything. He walked into the kitchen. Out of the corner of his eye he saw Ceiley looking at him, shaking off sleep, scared. He couldn't even pretend to crack a smile for her or show any sort of sign he was all right. He wasn't.

Esse followed him. "What happened?"

"Don't worry about it."

"Who did this to you?"

"No one."

"You're bleeding all over."

Ceiley had found her way into the entranceway, but stood back like he was some wild animal.

"I've never seen the likes," Esse said. "Let's get you cleaned up."

"Just let it be," he said, gritting his teeth. "I'm fine."

"Sure don't look it," she said.

Greer filled up a glass of water, drank it down.

"Does it hurt?" Ceiley asked from the doorway in a small voice. Her eyes were big and wide.

Everything hurts, he thought. Everything.

"Thanks for looking after my mom today," he managed.

"There are leftovers on the stove," Esse said. "Just fixed a little okra and butter beans, some cured ham."

He nodded absently.

"Want me to heat it up?"

"I just want to be alone," he said harshly.

Ceiley looked like she was going to cry.

"Well," Esse said, crossing her arms, "we'll just get out of your way then." She turned around and walked briskly out of the kitchen, scooting Ceiley along with her.

"Esse…" He trailed off. He didn't have the energy to be sorry for anything else tonight. He didn't even see them to the door.

Greer slumped into a chair, stared at a knife left on the table. He couldn't get his mind to slow down to think about any one thing. The room was silent. He almost wished for the sound of the leaky faucet again, something constant to focus on.

It could have been minutes or hours that he sat there; he didn't know. Everything was fractured, broken. Finally he got up and made his way to the bathroom. The small, cracked mirror that hung over the wash basin told a mean story: bits of skin hanging loose, scratches everywhere, dried blood. The thorns had gone to town on him, ripped him to shreds. He stared at his damaged reflection. For once the outside matched the ugliness of the inside.

The rubbing alcohol sat on a shelf he had built only last week. He dipped a corner of his towel into the antiseptic and brought the cloth to his face. The sting shot straight to the wound. Wound after wound after wound, sting after sting after sting, Greer disinfected his whole face, wiped his throat, his collarbone, his arms, his hands. It felt right almost, the pain. He could curl up in it, make a home there.

You ruined her life. Mrs. Thomas' words rang through his brain. *You killed everything.* That different kind of sting as her saliva hit his cheek. He rubbed alcohol across the spot, over and over again, as if he could wash clean the shame of it. But he knew: there's no wiping away shame.

Greer wanted a cigarette, but was so exhausted, he wasn't sure he even had the strength to bring his battered arm up to meet his mouth. But would it not, would not the blood from his busted lip make the smoke somehow sweeter?

He went to his room and laid down, not bothering to take his clothes off. It was a wonder the bed didn't collapse under him. No clock in the room, but he knew it was the deadest of night.

He turned onto his side, but quickly returned to his back. His face was so raw even pressing his skin against the soft pillow hurt. He vaguely thought of sitting up to take his shirt off; he felt sharp nettles still burrowing into his skin. Instead, he lay there, let them prick. The usual thoughts pricked, too: that first night in Snake Creek, the curve of Caroline's back, his father's narrowed eyes, headlights in the night. No matter how many miles he'd traveled or how many years passed, the same scenes always followed him. Again and again, he'd find himself in the woods at dusk, the encroaching darkness that enveloped him could roll in at any hour of day. Memories gnawed like gnats.

Now he had new fuel for his mind on fire. Mrs. Thomas' venom, strangers lit with hate. Would they track him down here or was Hickory far enough away?

We took care of it…How dare you?…No baby anymore.

In the moment's terror he hadn't fully absorbed Mrs. Thomas' words, but now they seeped in. Had Caroline carried his child? Aborted? What else could it mean.

His mind flashed back to their secret nights. Who had been thinking, being careful? Devastation covered Greer's face. He'd never felt so alone.

He slipped into a sleep without dreams. He did not toss or turn, but there wasn't a moment's rest in his slumber.

*   *   *

Greer woke early. Must have been only a few hours since he'd shut his eyes. Weariness still hung on him, but he knew there was no more sleep to be had. Like a machine, doing everything by rote, he went to the bathroom. Watched the stream of urine as he relieved himself. Splashed water on his face. It still stung. He felt hard as stone.

He went into the kitchen, made coffee. Lit a cigarette even though he knew not to smoke in the house. Who could call this a new day, yesterday already bleeding into this one? He stirred sugar in his coffee as the refrain played in his head. *Family. Damnation. Your family has brought nothing but damnation.*

He chugged the coffee down, even though it was too hot. He burned his tongue. He poured himself another cup. The coffee tasted bitter, no matter how much sugar he added.

The sun was just starting to rise. He walked to his mother's room, not sure if she would still be sleeping. She was already awake, though, her eyes open, gazing up at the ceiling. He came in and stood at the foot of her bed. He didn't raise his voice, but his words were firm: "We're going to the hospital," he said. "You're the only family I've got."

Elizabeth, who had never asked what he'd gotten up to these past few weeks as if it were no business of hers, looked at him with the calmest expression. She didn't even question the angry slashes across his face.

"All right then," she said, as if she'd been waiting for him to say that since day one.

TEN

(1977)

The cancer had spread everywhere. From some initial cells in her left breast, untold numbers now invaded Elizabeth's lymph nodes, populated her entire chest. It had metastasized to her lungs and bones, explaining her cough, her shortness of breath, the pain that seemed to pulse in the very marrow.

"How could you have let it go this long?" the doctor asked.

Neither Greer nor Elizabeth had an answer.

They looked at X-rays, tried to match her body to the bony images on transparent sheets. They listened to talk about malignancy and survival rates, learned that stage four of four was the farthest away from where you wanted to be.

Is it too late? Greer stared at what seemed a hologram with hundreds of white spots, a skeleton whose insides had sneezed sick cells. *How could he ask that? Was it too late?*

"In a case this advanced," the doctor said, "the only treatment options are aggressive. There will be radical side effects. Do you understand?"

Elizabeth didn't say anything, just nodded. Greer could see she didn't really understand.

"We have to do something, don't we?" he said.

"You should have done something a long time ago," the doctor said. They were sitting in old plastic chairs at Cooper Medical, still considered the "black hospital" even though that was all supposed to be past. Greer wondered if her care would have differed elsewhere.

"Well, we're here now," Greer said.

"There's no getting around a mastectomy," the doctor said. "And chemotherapy. But like I say, there's no guarantee."

"What do you think, Mama?" Greer asked.

"If you think we should do it, then we'll do it," Elizabeth said, speaking for the first time.

"Mama, it's not about me," he said.

"Do you want me to?"

Greer looked at her. Her eyes seemed to be asking something of him. "I'll be here," he said. "We'll fight."

"All right then," she said.

*   *   *

A week later, the waiting room was half-full with all types. A man next to him couldn't stop his foot from tapping up and down, a nervous sound that echoed around the room. Anytime someone got up to get a drink from the water fountain or pick up a new magazine from the table, or simply pace to pass the time, their shoes produced a shrill squeak against the floor. The room smelled of ammonia.

Some people seemed in a half-stupor, more bored than nervous, dulled from the wait. Like Greer, they'd been here many hours. There was only so long one could keep a constant tension.

Greer was used to waiting. Those many years working on cargo ships, he'd gotten used to what on the surface seemed monotonous. Nothing to see but sea. But he had learned there were plenty of ways to fill in the blank horizon. Watch the crest of the waves, measure the distance the birds flew above, follow the loop of thoughts that circled forever in his mind. Impatience was one of the few things that no longer afflicted him.

His mother had already successfully come out of surgery. He knew that much from the doctor's report a few hours ago. It would take time for the anesthesia to wear off and even then they would keep her for a few days.

When he was allowed to visit her, she was propped up in bed, wearing a thin gown, light green. From a certain angle he could see bandages across her chest. He shifted so he couldn't see.

"How are you feeling?" he asked.

"Don't know what it's supposed to feel like," she said.

"You look good, Mama."

Elizabeth chuckled, catching Greer by surprise. "I haven't looked good in years," she said.

"Doctor said it went well."

"If they say so. I wasn't awake to know."

Greer took a chair by her bed.

"We'll be able to get you home in a few days," he said. "You'll be more comfortable there."

"I'm fine, just fine."

"I've been getting things ready," he said.

"What things?"

"Oh, I don't know. Just things to make it easier." Maybe he shouldn't have said anything. She'd see for herself when she got home: the railing he'd put next to the bed, the sink he'd brought higher so she didn't have to bend over as much.

"Well," she said, "not sure why anything would be harder. Just without one of these." She motioned vaguely towards her chest.

Greer looked away, embarrassed, then back at her. "I'm really sorry, Mama. It was the only chance."

She shook her head a little. "I've been losing pieces of myself my whole life," she said. "Somehow I'm still here."

"You are," he said. "And you'll get through this, too."

"We'll see how it goes." She lay her head back, closed her eyes.

Yes, they'd see.

In a way, Greer was almost relieved that this was about all he'd be able to see to for a while.

*   *   *

They'd been in the bathroom an hour, Elizabeth curled up on the floor near the toilet, Greer crouched down next to her. She'd asked him to help her in here, so she could rest next to the commode, ready for the coming onslaught she sensed would stay awhile. A blanket Greer laid down softened the hard tile, though these days little prevented her from feeling all bone.

The first time Elizabeth threw up, she hadn't made it out of bed. So scared of the violence rising from her body, she kept trying to will it down. Of course, there was no way to stop it. A thin green bile mixed with that morning's porridge made its way onto the duvet. Greer took the cover and washed it without complaint.

It soon became clear the waves of nausea would recur often. She was beginning to know which would be extended episodes.

"Here comes another," she said.

Greer lifted his mother over the toilet bowl, placed his hand to support her head while she threw up. He felt her whole body shake, doing what a body does—trying to rid itself of poison inside.

"I can't breathe," she said, in between convulsions.

"You're breathing, Mama. You're all right. Why don't you lie down again?"

"Right here," she said. Greer lowered her back to the bathroom floor.

"I've told you, why don't you rest in bed? We have a bucket."

"You shouldn't have to keep cleaning up my mess."

"It's ok. You can't help it."

Elizabeth seemed to run both hot and cold. He wiped sweat from her forehead, but she was reaching for the other blanket to cover herself up again. Sometimes she couldn't stop shivering.

"Maybe you've been cleaning up my mess for a while," she said.

Greer didn't say anything. He flushed the toilet. The water had turned a sickly brown. It didn't matter how many times he flushed anymore, the water never seemed clean.

"Yes, wash it down the drain," she said. "Just flush it down." He flushed again, but the water stayed cloudy.

"Is this worse?" Greer began. When he had come home, he could see that she was already far gone with her sickness. Even the lump had grown so big you could tell that the breast had swelled. Watching the way she suffered now, though, he had to wonder if they'd done the right thing.

"Is what worse?" she said. "I thought you said to fight."

"Yes," he said. "Fight."

"Do you still want me to? Or maybe it doesn't matter. You didn't need me for so long."

Greer never talked about what he needed. He'd survived for years without that. He said only, "It matters, Mama."

"If you say so, baby." She closed her eyes and didn't speak for a long time. He couldn't tell if she was sleeping or not until she spoke again. "Imagine if we still had the outhouse."

"What's that, Mama?"

"All kinds of weather, didn't matter."

"It must have been really different." His mother had never talked much about growing up.

"My daddy wouldn't have believed a toilet like this in the house. Lucky it's here now."

"Yes." He waited to see if she'd share anything more. When she didn't, he added, "There are still plenty of places in the world with outhouses. You'd think time had stopped still."

"Mmm," Elizabeth said. "Sometimes I wish time had stopped still."

"When, Mama?" When would she have wanted to freeze time?

Elizabeth rolled onto her side. "I didn't even know you could be this sick."

He shifted the pillow under her head. "You'll get your sea legs," he said.

"Sea legs?"

"Hopefully you'll get used to the treatment."

"I don't want sea legs."

"It's just an expression."

"Strange," she said. "It's got nothing to do with my legs."

"I know." He remembered the lurching of his stomach he thought impossible to get used to. But you can get used to almost anything. Maybe they both knew that.

"Did I ever tell you?" she said. "I wanted to go to Europe."

"No," he said. "You didn't tell me."

Elizabeth tried to prop herself on her elbow. Greer helped her. "I can't," she said, holding onto the toilet bowl.

"Yes you can," he said. "It comes on its own."

She threw up. When he lay her back down, all the wind seemed knocked out of her. It was too bad; he wanted to know more. Europe? He had never thought of his mother as having dreams, anything other than her sadness. A strange solace as she only grew sicker, but in some ways she seemed slowly to be coming alive.

ELEVEN

(1977)

When Ceiley had run away last month—Greer had obviously filled her head with too many stories too soon—he had felt relief to have found her, did not want to be responsible for sending such an unprepared girl out into the world. Still, he quietly championed her. Had he rescued her by bringing her back—or by giving her the courage to go?

Since that night he'd come back broken and bruised, though, it was as if she was too afraid to talk to him. She barely glanced his way. He didn't stray too far from home these days, keeping close by his mother's side—and if he were honest, still shaken from that night, too—but on his breaks out on the porch, cigarette in hand, he'd seen her scurrying away if she caught sight of him. He could understand—how often had he wanted to run away from himself? He'd have to make it up to her somehow.

"Ceiley," he called out to her.

She stopped and seemed to hesitate on the road.

"Off to the library?" he asked.

She nodded, warily.

"Hey, why don't you come talk to me for a minute?" he said.

"They'll be closing soon," she said, though it wasn't true.

Greer went out to meet her in the street. "Well, how about I walk you then? I need to stretch my legs anyway."

"If you want," she said, shrugging.

"How's school going?" he asked.

"Going."

Greer finished his cigarette, stubbed it out on the ground. "Look, Ceiley, I'm sorry about the other night. I didn't mean to snap at y'all."

She didn't say anything, but he could tell she was listening.

"It's just been hard being back," he said.

"You looked like someone had slapped fireweed across your face."

"Not too far off," he said.

"What were you doing?" she said.

Greer sighed. What had he been doing? "I don't know. Trying to get some answers. When maybe there aren't any."

"Well, what's the question? Shouldn't you start there?"

"That's a good point."

Ceiley tugged on the straps of her backpack.

"Heavy?" Greer said. "Want me to take it?"

"No," she said. "Just need to drop off these books."

"Read anything good?"

"*Go Tell It On the Mountain.*"

"Wow, you reading Baldwin already?"

They passed Wilson's. He gave a cursory wave.

"I do miss talking to you, Ceiley."

"Really?"

"You're a smart kid."

"Oh." She fell silent again. Then, "I guess I really am a kid."

"Nothing wrong with that," he said. "Sometimes wish I didn't have to grow up myself."

"No use pining after things that are no longer green," Ceiley said.

Greer gave her a quizzical look. "What's that from?" he said.

"You," she said. "You told me that."

"Hmm," he said. "Guess I did."

"Don't know what it means, but it sounds about right."

They were in front of the library now, the one-room house that called itself one, in any case.

"Well, here you are, little lady," he said. "Hope you find some good books. You can come by and tell me about them later, if you want."

Ceiley pulled at her backpack strap again, hesitated before going. "Greer?"

"Yeah?"

"When I ran away, I didn't really know what I was doing. I'm glad you came and got me."

"And I'm glad I found you."

"Bannen's boring, but it sure seems scary out there. You didn't tell me that part."

"Oh, I don't know. When you're older you might still want to go somewhere. When you're ready," he said.

"Look at what happened to you."

Was she referring to the other night? She'd have no way of knowing anything else. Would she? "It's funny," he said. "It's not really what happened out there that messed me up."

"Messed you up?"

Greer laughed, a sad laugh. "Oh, never mind. Go on and get some books. I'll see you later."

"Ok," she said. "Maybe you need some better stories, too."

Greer pulled out another cigarette. "You're always thinking."

*   *   *

Ceiley did come back later that evening, her excitement taking over any reluctance she might have had. Returning from the library she turned toward his house rather than her own when she saw him sitting on the porch, starting to speak before she was even up to his steps.

"You know the light we see from stars is from a *million* years ago? The star might not even *be* there even though we're looking right at it?"

Greer smiled. "Yeah, I think I heard something about that."

"And there are planets that have rings and they're made of ice and stone," she said, barely stopping to catch her breath. "And sometimes they have their own moon? And these things are so far away we have to talk about them in light years? And that year has nothing to do with time, it's six trillion miles."

Greer motioned for her to sit down. "Slow down there, lady, throwing facts at me left and right," he said chuckling.

Ceiley pulled a book out of her knapsack, ignoring his gesture. *Amazing Astronomy!* It had a picture of a supernova deep in a black sky.

"That's some exciting stuff," Greer said.

Ceiley gave an embarrassed smile. Her body seemed to fold up in on itself. "Well, I don't know, maybe it's stupid. I just didn't know any of that before."

Greer shook his head. "Hey, not stupid at all. I used to stare at the sky all the time when I was sailing."

"Just makes you feel like the world is big, you know?" she said, standing straighter again. "Like even from right here I can look up and see something amazing. I didn't even *know* what I was seeing before."

"Told you, kid, you have to look up."

She smirked. "Yeah, but that's not what you were talking about. You don't know *everything*."

Greer raised his hands in mock defeat. "You got me there."

"Anyway, just found this book in the library today. Got no one else to tell," she mumbled at the end.

Greer took the book and flipped through it. Galaxies, solar systems, dwarf stars. He handed it back to her. "So your mama did right," he said.

Ceiley screwed up her face skeptically. "What do you mean?"

"Naming you Celestial. Astronomy's the study of celestial bodies. Fits you perfectly."

"Huh," Ceiley said, putting the book back in her sack. "Didn't think about it like that."

"Well, just saying she might be smarter than you think."

"Huh," she said again, this time in a tone that sounded like *that* might win as the day's most unbelievable discovery. "Well, anyway, I gotta get home for dinner. See you around."

"Sure thing," he said.

He watched her bound across the street, her backpack bouncing up and down. Mosquitoes were coming out now; they always seemed to swarm most at dusk. He'd go in soon, too. It was nice having her company again, he thought. She provided some energy and light in the midst of the gloom.

And it was true, what he'd told her. He'd gaze up at the constellations when he was out at sea. That infinite sky to which he'd pose questions. All those questions, the same ones over and over again. She brought up a good point: What was visible might not even exist anymore. He'd spent most of his life dealing in the opposite—the invisible, palpable and real. He'd always thought of it in terms of silent scars, but maybe there was a positive angle, too. You couldn't see gravity, yet it held us all to the ground. Somehow, even with all its chaos, the universe kept itself from simply falling apart.

*   *   *

Esse came to see him the next day, a green bean casserole in hand. "Thought you might be tired of cooking," she said.

"That's thoughtful, Esse. Thank you." Greer opened the door and let her in, took the dish off her hands. "Can I get you something to drink? Sweet tea?"

"No, I'm fine, not staying long. I'm not interrupting, am I?"

"No," he said. "Just fixing some stuff around the house. My mama's sleeping."

Esse nodded absently.

"Please, sit," he said ushering her into the living room. "I'm glad you stopped by. I didn't get a chance to apologize properly for the other night. That was kind, you looking after Mama when I had to go out. Then I just came home like that."

"Oh, that's all right," she said, tapping her foot up and down. Her eyes wandered around the room; they couldn't seem to settle on any one thing. Greer wondered why she was so distracted.

"How are you getting along these days, Esse?"

"Same old, same old," she said. "Getting ready for a big bake sale at the church. Cleaning. Trying to keep that girl of mine out of trouble."

"Oh, Ceiley's not going to get into any trouble. She's a good kid."

Esse stopped tapping her foot and looked at him finally. "Well, that's what I wanted to talk to you about."

"Oh?"

"I saw you two talking yesterday out in the road."

"Yeah. I was walking her to the library. She stopped over on her way back."

Esse shook her head. "I just don't know what it is you want from her. She's only a little girl."

"I don't want anything, Esse," Greer said, surprised.

"Doesn't seem right to me, a man your age talking to a girl all the time."

"Now wait a minute, Esse. What are you trying to say?"

"That's it. I just went and said it."

Greer leaned back in his chair. "I'm sorry she ran away, but I went and got her. She's not looking to do that again."

"I'm grateful to you for that. For going and finding her. But it was your fault she left in the first place."

Greer blew out a rush of air. "Everything's my fault, right?"

"I'm just saying, watch out. I'm watching you. You blow

back into town. Put notions into a little girl's head. Come back that night acting all crazy. I just don't know."

"God damn," he said. "Does everyone think I'm just going around trying to ruin people's lives?"

She flinched. "There's no need to use language like that."

"You know, Esse, I may be a bastard, but I'm not that kind of a bastard."

She didn't say anything.

"I think you might be lumping me in with someone you shouldn't be lumping me in with."

Esse got up. "I shouldn't have said anything."

"No, sit down," Greer said. "Really. People can't talk about anything around here. You came for a reason."

"She's my baby."

"And you're afraid I'm doing something with her? Is that it?"

"I didn't say that," she said, clearly uncomfortable.

"Well, I can assure you, that's the furthest thing from my mind." He gave a short, ironic laugh. "The furthest."

Esse clasped, then unclasped her hands before making herself stop fidgeting. "We're simple people around here. I don't know anything about what you're bringing back."

Greer looked at her for a moment. Her hair pulled back tight with oversized bobby pins, the faintest of circles under her eyes, darker, yet more translucent, than her dark skin. Her face largely untouched by lines retained hints of youth, but a seriousness stole what by all rights should have still been hers at her age. He knew the feeling. They weren't that old yet, were they?

"You know, Esse, I think Bannen's been bad to both of us. I saw you. I remember back then." He could see her jaw clench.

"I'm really sorry for whatever happened to you. Men aren't supposed to do that. Not all men are like that."

Esse bit her lower lip, looked to the side. She didn't say anything for a while and Greer thought it best to just let the words hang there as long as they needed to. She glanced back at him, then back down at her hands. "You never did seem like you belonged here."

"Well, that may be something we can agree on."

They sat in silence for a few minutes.

"You're just looking after your daughter," Greer said. "I can respect that."

"I know you never did do anyone no harm," she said softly. "That I knew. Just looking out is all."

Greer's mind flitted to Caroline, to her mother, to Gloria. People had been hurt in his wake. Did it make any difference that he'd never intended any harm?

"She's a special kid."

"She's a child of God."

Greer nodded. He wondered, did she really still believe that old story? Everyone had supported it, confirmed even by the town doctor. But did mythmaking actually help?

"You have every reason to love her," he said.

"She clung to you, soon as you came back," Esse said. "Feels like she doesn't want to be anywhere near me."

"Kids need space. It's the age."

"I always wondered if she needed a father. I've never let a man come within two miles of me."

He could swear he saw tears gathering in her eyes, though she kept them there. "I can understand that," he said. "It's a lot for you to bear."

After a moment, Esse rose. "Well, I'll be going now. You let me know if Miss Elizabeth needs any more help. I've not always been the best neighbor."

"We're getting along just fine," he said. "Thank you, though."

Esse wavered at the door.

"Something else?" he said.

"No," she said, though it wasn't all that convincing.

"Ok, well, right across the street if you think of anything."

She nodded then turned to go, before turning back again. "Ceiley did tell me you said I'd done right. By her name, I mean."

"Oh, yeah," he said swiping his hand across the back of his neck. "Creative."

"Well, thank you for saying that anyway. It got her talking to me at least a little bit."

"Well, I'm glad. No need to thank me for that," he said.

Greer watched her cross the road and disappear into her bungalow, then he went inside and sat down on the couch again. The women in this town, he thought. Had every single one of them been hurt? Was there anyone walking around without wounds?

When he brought soup into Elizabeth that night, she told him she felt like her entire throat had closed up and she didn't feel hungry in the least. It was true. When he tried feeding her, she couldn't swallow even a single spoonful; it only ended up on her chin. So he just sat there with her until the room grew dark. Neither of them moved to turn on a light. He watched until she nodded off, stoic even in sleep. Greer didn't believe in miracles like some people. But maybe he wished he could.

TWELVE (THE RAINBOW)

(1944 / 1977)

Every note has its own color. Each sound a new flavor on the tongue. Picture pitch, pull it near. Breathe in the song, its full-bodied smell.

"You are all senses," he said. "Every part of me tingles when you're near."

She smiled as a warm summer storm rumbled around them, rain fell down.

"You're a rainbow, my sweet. Cut through the clouds. Wash them away."

She ran her hands over his chocolate skin, wiped away the clear droplets clinging to his face, cheeks, throat. Of course any element on earth would want to be that close to him. Seep into his pores.

Usually she would run for shelter during a storm. But he was her shelter; no need to run. The whole world seemed to hold them, them alone, like a sky cradles stars, like the lone lantern on a country road at night, the only light, all light contained there.

He wrapped his arms around her, the embrace she always craved.

But then he slid his hand into the crook under her arm, began to wiggle his fingers back and forth, making her body jerk this way and that, trying to refuse, but at the same time amused by the tickling touch.

She giggled, first a little, then a lot, doubled over in pain from the laughter. A happy pain.

"I love every sound you make," he said, laughing himself, unrelenting, grazing his fingers where a soft fuzz grew.

"Major, stop it," she swatted at him, delighted. "Clayton Major!"

They laughed a full orchestra. A symphony. She couldn't stop.

"Mama?"

Heehee. Stop. Teehee. Stop it. (Don't stop).

"Mama, are you ok?"

Elizabeth slowly opened her eyes, not yet seeing anything in the dark, but feeling a body hovering over her, a cold compress on her forehead.

"You were tossing and turning," Greer said. "Making a lot of noise."

His face was beginning to come into focus. It was scrunched up in concern, a thick vertical line between his two eyebrows.

"Sometimes, good memories greet me when I sleep," she said.

"Oh." Greer's face relaxed. "That's nice, Mama."

He removed the cloth from her forehead; she seemed to be sweating less now.

Good memories while she slept? Greer found little solace in sleep. That was where the nightmares lurked.

But this, was that her sound of happiness? Had it really been laughter he had heard?

"What's the prettiest rainbow you ever saw?" Elizabeth asked him.

Greer blinked. "Rainbow?"

"I was just thinking about how I never paid enough attention to things like rainbows. But they're amazing, aren't they?"

Greer nodded. He'd seen rainbows fill the sky from many different corners of the world. Nothing compared to seeing the colorful arc over the wide open sea.

"They are," he said. "The bending of the sun's rays inside raindrops."

"Is that what makes them?" she asked. She tried to lift herself up a little, but the effort didn't get her much higher.

"It's still early, Mama. Not even dawn. Sure you want to get up now?"

"Inside raindrops? I didn't learn enough in my time. A rainbow," she said, shaking her head from side to side. But she seemed, yes. She seemed almost carefree.

"It's never too late, is it?" Greer asked, unsure himself.

Elizabeth smiled. "I guess we'd better hope that it's not." She turned on her side. "You been here the whole night?"

Greer nodded, cocked his head toward the rocking chair.

"Go on and get some real sleep, baby. I'll get back to dreaming, too."

CLAYTON MAJOR MICHAELS

(beyond time)

Her voice had come from a distance; it made me feel both near and far. I had traveled the long road from Florida where my hands had smelled of citrus, to arrive in time for another state's harvest. I've lain in many states now, though everything seems to run together: the changing landscape, the shifting seasons. Elizabeth and I found a state of grace together, but it was hard watching her after, humming beneath a willow tree, her breath harsh and haggard.

Georgia's sweet potato harvest begins in late summer, but I took my time getting up there. A town named Bannen and a river that cut it in two. There was little motivation to hurry, even though I depended on those well-worn trails. Get on one path, pick, pick up, pick again.

When I arrived, the air still held summer's high humidity even though it was past. On a rare day off, I followed the thin river for miles. It started to grow in width, and then I heard Elizabeth. I heard her before I saw her. The notes so clear I thought I could see through them. They pierced right through the wet air.

When I saw her, I immediately felt a thirst. Sometimes one person can change everything you thought you knew about yourself and the world. She faced the river as if it were an audience. The water must have delighted in such a fine performance. She wore a yellow sundress dotted with purple flowers; the cloth clung loosely to her frame. A breeze lifted the knee-length dress and revealed her slender thighs, a lighter brown than her calves. Like honey. I count myself a lucky man that I had many occasions to run my hands over those legs.

There were purple flowers along the bank of the river too. This is what it always felt like with her—perfect. Fragile, too, or maybe that was just me, never able to stay in one place, set down roots, care about anything because it might hurt to get attached. So instead I'd tell jokes, wouldn't take anything seriously. That's what I mean, though. I took Elizabeth seriously. First time in my life. The funnyman.

I sang out to her, a line of harmony to the familiar church hymn, and she stopped singing and turned quickly. I walked towards her evenly, singing the whole time, and nodded my head, looking her straight in the eye. She stood still for a minute, but soon opened her mouth again, hesitantly at first, then as full-bodied as before.

And that's how it was from then on. Our love came quick, all at once, right then, though we took our time in loving each other. In our caresses. Picnics in grass, whispering and stroking —all the things young lovers do, all day we did. We talked of running away. We'd have to cross an ocean to do that. This seemed appropriate, our love by the banks of a river. She had heard of a man from Curryville who sang for kings and queens in Europe but was spat on here. Arrested in Rome, Georgia, but the toast of Rome, Italy. They called him Mister Hayes over there. I won't repeat what they called him here. Plenty called me those things, too. Like water off my back, that's what I had to let it be.

She could barely read, but she kept the newspaper clipping in her change purse. You see how it is, she'd say. You see how it could be. If only we could get out.

Elizabeth was royalty to me. I said, *Liz Bet, bet you could do that, too, sing for kings and queens if you wanted to.* She had talent. We all have talent; some of us choose to ignore it or are kept from it. Or hide it or doubt it till it grows feeble and dies. My talent was loving that woman, but sometimes I fear I did my job too well—she never let me go. *Liz Bet, bet you don't know how much I love you.* She did, though, from the looks of it.

I've wanted to tell her you can't blame a river for running. That I hear her, not from a place we call heaven, but the land that I tilled all my life. Her salty tears entered the fresh water of Sicama River. Hissing accusations hurled at the water. As if she were the one drowned. Like her lungs filled.

There is no time here, but I've watched her through the changes. As her belly swelled with a child not mine, a light-skinned boy with my family name.

I don't mind. If I couldn't hold her in the water, in the breeze, would I do anything different? On the other side, my insides would have been torn. I would have gone blind with pain. I hid my faults from her, but deep down, I was a jealous man. She made me want to be better. Here, in this place unnamed, all that exists is love. It's hard to tell if that's what she was seeking herself. I am the hole in the ground, and the cloud about to release rain.

Her hair has grown wiry and her voice has grown hoarse. I want to tell her the world doesn't want you to stay hidden; nothing is beautiful that way. I want to tell her "Sing, Elizabeth." That was our mating call. "Sing, Major," she would say, and I would make up a song.

The river seems wider at night, the water so black it competes with the dark sky holding its stars. It was getting on to fall, the late autumn air crisp. She dared me to go into the river. She'd never say it, but she always tested the limits of my love.

The water was cold. Everything seems simple now. Hot, cold, here, there, no, yes. Life is made up of simple choices. We pile them together and think it's complicated.

"Come on out here, baby," I said.

"You crazy," she said, though she was already stepping in to meet me. "Yeah, that's why you love me." I think it was. I made her feel free, though I know we never truly were. We weren't allowed to be.

"Sing, Major," she said, still ankle deep.

"*My baby splashes, my baby dashes, my baby has the prettiest eyelashes, when she gives me a wink, I just can't think, I could die happy with her.*"

I had moved to the center of the river. "Major Michaels, at your service, ma'am," I called out.

The last thing I heard was her laugh.

Life doesn't flash before your eyes as they say, though it's amazing the things you can see clearly through what might otherwise be chaos. I saw the way the moon gleamed on her body, the branches of the trees being tousled by the wind, my pile of clothes lying on the bank. I could not speak, but as I saw her move toward me in the water, I tried to tell her no.

*   *   *

The skin of a Georgia Jet sweet potato is so red it almost looks purple. I told her this once. That something can be so deep it appears as something else. I've always wanted to remind her of that. It must have echoed out across the water somehow. *No.* I was a jealous man, but not a selfish one. As she entered the river, I wanted to stop her from risking herself. *The current is too swift, too hard, you'll fall.* Your mind races and you think words and you see images flying at you: purple flowers, yellow sun, her brown nipples, my rough hands on them, the moon, the stars, everything falling, grasping, pulling, spinning. No. I have watched her through these years, and I don't think that's what she understood as I struggled up against the water. How can I tell her blame serves no one. *It was not your fault.* No.

It's a waste, her silence. Live it, live it, I've wanted to say. She used to sing gospel so gorgeous she could have made nonbelievers fall to their knees. Then she lost her religion. What was left? I want to tell her, so much. So much more, baby. Heavy with guilt. She would have sunk down into the river if she had ever dared to step in it again. I wanted to say, but we are so light, we are air. Isn't it incredible? You can't hold water. It runs free. I release you.

Liz Bet, sing, lover. She didn't hear me for the longest time.

But I see she is starting to as she gets closer.

Don't be afraid, Liz Bet. Come this way.

THIRTEEN

(1977)

Who could have imagined that as her throat grew scratchy and her body wasted away, Elizabeth would start to let the words flow? As if some invisible countdown had begun and there was a limited time to speak, she just started talking. She told Greer about her parents, how they were sharecroppers until they managed to buy a better level of freedom—nothing short of a miracle in those days.

She told him she determined to get herself a cleaning job rather than pick cotton because she could never avoid the burrs. Even working at her hardest, her hands didn't bleed from pushing a mop. She spoke about practicing vocal scales amidst a scrub clearing and making jam from wild blueberries that grew at the edge of the fields.

She asked him about everywhere he'd been, places she'd never once heard of and wouldn't ever even see on a map. The farthest she'd traveled was from the bottomlands to East Bannen, but she'd seen whole towns empty of their colored folks when she'd passed through. "Up North things were different," she said. Somehow Bannen had missed the great migration.

"You used to sleepwalk when you were younger," she said. This was news to Greer. She said it seemed fitting that he had ended up wandering all over the land.

"How did you get to be such a good man?"

They were back in the hospital now, waiting for the doctor to come back with reports from a new round of tests. Why couldn't she eat? What could be done?

"What?" Greer said, taken aback.

"You're a good man. And I know I didn't have much to do with that," she said.

Greer looked stricken. "I don't know why you're saying that."

"You are, baby. You're all grown up. And you came back for me. Look at you." Greer wondered what she saw when she looked at him. "Could you get me some more water?" she asked, giving a slight nod to her empty cup beside the bed.

"Sure," he said, relieved at something to do. He went into the hospital corridor. There was a water fountain just at the end of the hall. He watched the graceful arc of the water as he filled the little plastic cup, then stood against the wall for a moment, trying to gather himself. Doctors in their long white coats passed by, residents in their green scrubs. No one paid him any mind.

A good man? He thought about how he had grown up thinking of men as some shadow population, how he yearned to be real. And yet, he had become a shadow, too, somehow. He'd look in mirrors sometimes, just to make sure he was still there.

Greer went back to his mother's room feeling heavy. She reached out for the cup and held on to his hand.

"I used to sing to you when you were little. I know you don't remember it," she said.

Greer shook his head, confused. "I don't remember…"

She let go of his hand and took a long drink. "Well, I'd hum to you. I guess it wasn't really singing."

"I really don't remember that," he said again.

"Sometimes it was the only way to get you to quiet down. You always were wanting something, and I never knew what to give you. It was just you and me and sometimes I didn't know what to do."

"You were alone," he said, and it sunk in, though he had always known it.

"I should have talked to you more then. You liked my voice."

Greer nodded.

"Your father," she said, and Greer's heart quickened, "I wouldn't have been able to raise you without his help," she said. "I needed that money. He gave you those books."

Greer felt his throat tighten.

"I never thought not telling you would make you go away. I was trying to keep you safe."

Greer shook his head. "Why are you telling me all of this today?"

"I didn't mean for it to be like that," she said.

"I know," and he did know. How could he tell her that he was beginning to understand that she had needed to hold onto Major for some reason, to make that her story? What it would mean for his own life, how could she ever have guessed?

"I just wanted to keep you safe. I tried my best," she said.

Greer felt tears building up behind his eyes, but he tried to keep them at bay. "The truth might have kept us safe," he said.

"I know that now, baby. I'm sorry. Oh," she said. "Don't cry. I didn't mean to make you cry."

"It's ok," Greer said.

"Mr. Thomas, I don't know what he would have done if I told you sooner, but maybe I should have. He did ask after you from time to time."

Greer couldn't help it now, the tears rolled down his face.

"Why don't you come over here?" she said. Elizabeth opened her thin arms to him, and after a brief pause, he let himself fall into them. He felt her small arms pull him tight. Those fragile arms, yet she felt stronger than he did at the moment.

"Don't leave, Mama," he said.

"My baby," she said, and they sat there like that for a long time, mother and son, held in an embrace that tried spanning too many years.

*   *   *

When Greer got home that night, he fell into his childhood bed, exhausted. He looked at the books lined up against the wall—they were still there, just as they were when he left. Nothing in his room had been touched, like it had been frozen in time. Like he was still sixteen.

But he wasn't.

He replayed all that his mother had said today. If he had known the truth sooner, *would* he have been kept safe from all that followed? Who would he be if he hadn't looked for his father, loved Caroline, left? A good man? That question always tormented him.

Greer closed his eyes, felt his weight sink into the old mattress. He pictured himself as a man without anchor, adrift on open seas. Who would he have left in the world if his mother passed?

He didn't bother to take his clothes off that night, his long-sleeved shirt, black trousers. He always dressed formally, but right now he could care less if the fabric wrinkled, if the clothes would need a good dry-clean.

He lay still on the bed, dressed in that suit fit for a wake, and fell into a sleep so deep he wasn't sure he'd ever return.

*   *   *

The sound of the telephone woke him with a start. He realized he hadn't once heard the phone ring in this house. No one knew the number, for one thing. Elizabeth had never had a phone before Greer finally bought one. He'd explained it was a connection to the world, times were changing. He didn't tell her it was also because it made him feel less lonely at first, nor admit later it was also because he was afraid.

That's why he knew the ringing phone, at this early hour, could only mean bad news. He'd given the number to the hospital; that was all.

He hurried out of his room, then stopped short before the phone sitting there so unassuming on the living room side table, that cruel object unaware of the gravity of the call it carried. He didn't want to hear it, whatever it was. He wasn't ready.

But what had life taught him? What had he learned? There was no shifting the terms. The truth still existed, even if you were never told.

"Hello?" he said, cradling the cold receiver against his ear. The caller had been patient. At least fifteen rings had gone by.

"Mr. Michaels?" a woman's voice asked.

"Yes," he said.

"This is Cooper Medical calling. I'm afraid we have some bad news."

"Yes." How strange it was—saying yes to acknowledge something, when really all you wanted to say was no.

"If you could come on down to the hospital as soon as you can, that'd be best."

"What happened?"

"It's your mother, sir."

"Of course it's my mother, damn it. Why else would you be calling?" Anger pushed the words out of his mouth before he could stop them.

"I know it's a stressful time," the woman said. Greer wondered which nurse this was. Had he ever seen her? She had a kind voice, and kind wasn't a word he'd normally use about their experience at the hospital.

"Can you tell me what happened or am I supposed to guess?"

"Mr. Michaels, I'm very sorry to inform you that your mother passed away during the night."

Greer didn't say anything.

"Sir?"

Silence.

"Mr. Michaels? Hello?"

"Yes."

"You might like to get down here as fast as you can. See her now before she's moved."

There was a long pause. "Sir?" she asked again.

"But how did this happen?" Greer asked. "I spoke to her just hours ago," he said. *She held me in her arms; she was stronger than I was.*

"It was a peaceful end," the woman said.

"I thought she'd just gotten worse. I didn't think you were going to say that."

"It's always a shock."

Greer stayed on the line for a second, listening to the woman breathe. Then he let the phone slide from his ear. He carefully replaced it into the receiver. He vaguely felt bad hanging up on her, but there was nothing to say.

*   *   *

They hadn't warned him. He'd gotten used to Elizabeth's changing appearance—the weight she lost, her head covered in colorful scarves when her hair began falling out in clumps. But he didn't know that a human body could transform into a skeleton overnight. That death fled with more than just life. It took away a person's shape, the roundness of cheeks, only skin stretched over bone left behind.

"This isn't her," he said.

A nurse nodded empathetically—the same one on the phone? "You were close?" she asked.

Close. How to answer the question? They had been close to getting there. Just starting.

"What happens now?"

He only half listened as they walked him through the next steps. People did this every day, when they had never done it before. How did you suddenly know who to call to transport the body to the morgue, that you must visit the funeral parlor, pick out a casket, decide on a headstone, order flowers?

What happens now. He hadn't meant it like that; not a question of the many details to deal with. Logistics.

He meant: What happens. What now? She was gone.

He felt hollow, which for once, was probably the best way to feel. It made him efficient. He could get swept along in the preparations.

It was only when they gave him Elizabeth's belongings to take home with him that night that he cried. Her small change purse contained a tube of lipstick (he'd never seen her wear lipstick), a meager assortment of coins, and one newspaper clipping, faded and yellow with age.

"Georgia Negro sings in Europe," the headline read. A small black and white photo, the face hardly discernible, with a caption: *"Roland Hayes from Curryville, Georgia."* It was a short article, but it said enough.

Greer looked at it for a long time, then folded the article back up. Tucked it into his journal.

"Tell me about Europe," Elizabeth had asked him. He remembered the one time he had heard her sing; people compared it to the sound of angels.

I hope she gets her dream now, he thought, to anyone who might be up there listening.

FOURTEEN

(1977)

Ceiley picked up the recorder, placed her fingers in the grooves, and blew. The primer music book in front of her was open to "Für Elise" and she followed the round notes as they climbed up and down the staff. She loved reading this new language, these marks like black raindrops with flags.

Esse had let her join the band for the start of the new school year and she was still getting used to the instrument before moving to a more complicated woodwind: the nimble fingering, the correct amount of air to send through its shell. Though Ceiley's first attempts had produced nothing more than squeaks—shrill, reedy complaints—she had learned to control her breath and make clear, pure sounds.

She set the recorder down, though, too distracted today to practice. She looked out the window again, as she'd been doing all day. A steady stream of people had been trickling in and out of Greer's house since yesterday afternoon, but she hadn't seen him all day, not even to step foot outside for a cigarette break. She wondered if he'd smoke inside, now that Miss Elizabeth was gone.

Smells from the kitchen wafted into the living room and Ceiley realized she was ravenous. She'd kept vigil since the morning, watching for Greer, wondering what he was doing or feeling inside that house. All alone, without his mother.

Her eyes pricked a little, and she told herself it was just Esse's cooking, the cayenne peppers her mother often used to spice up a dish.

Esse had set to cooking as soon as she'd heard the news. "It's what you do," she'd said.

Ceiley was surprised at her mother's sudden knowledge. Certain of the rituals. Sure in the proper motions. Without prompting, she'd quietly started preparing meals for Greer, went to help him with arrangements.

How did she know what to do? Ceiley wondered, then remembered—as she didn't often enough—that her mother had lost her own parents, too. She had done all this before.

Ceiley picked up the recorder again, but this time the notes were off, her lungs not full enough of wind.

"Celestial, stop that blowing for a minute and come on in here," her mother called. "Take this on over." She handed Ceiley a casserole covered in tin foil, the heat still rising nonetheless.

Esse's apron was splattered with a red sauce, but other than that she was well-put together. Assured. Calm.

"Aren't we bothering him?" Ceiley asked.

"It's better to have people around," Esse said. "He needs that right now."

Ceiley stood there a minute longer, though the casserole was growing heavy in her arms. "What's he feeling?" she asked. "I mean, what am I supposed to say?"

Esse stopped and looked at her with such gentleness it almost took Ceiley's breath away.

"It's not the words that matter so much. He's feeling lots of things." She wiped her hands on her apron. "There used to be so much silence when someone died, like you weren't supposed to talk none. That's hard." She laid a hand on Ceiley's shoulder. "It's just a comfort you're there. Go on now. I'll bring over dessert later." She turned and opened the oven where a pie was baking inside.

Ceiley stared at her mother for a second, bent at the waist, efficient, then left the kitchen with the hot meal in hand. Things were changing between them. So slow she hadn't noticed at first, but then she did. Esse becoming more of a mystery to her, more interesting, the more she talked.

Ceiley knocked on Greer's door, hoping no one else would be in there, but half hoping the opposite, too. That'd take the pressure off if there were other guests. When he opened the door, though, it was just him.

"Oh, Ceiley," he said, "a real familiar face." He held the door open for her.

She walked in, but not before noting his bloodshot eyes, his weary air. He still gave her his smile, though, sad as it was. She walked straight to the kitchen and gave a short laugh, then cut it off, embarrassed.

"That's all right," he said. "It *is* pretty funny. How am I supposed to eat all this myself?"

The counters were lined with dishes, in pots, in pans, in containers of all sizes.

"That's what you do," she said, echoing her mother.

"Looks like it," Greer said. "How 'bout we eat what you brought, though? Is it your mom's green bean casserole? That sure was good."

Ceiley didn't know what she was carrying, actually. She folded the tin foil back. "Marinated chicken," she said. "Has cayenne pepper, it's hot."

"Great," Greer said, then slumped into a chair. He rested his face in his hand. Ceiley didn't know if she should go, but she remembered her mother's words, that it was a comfort to him she was there. She'd just have to trust her mother that was true.

Ceiley opened the cupboard and pulled out two plates, dished out the food onto them. She spied someone else's potato salad and thought that'd go well with it, too. She placed the plate in front of Greer, got a couple of forks, then sat down herself.

"Thanks, Ceiley," he said, picking up his fork, but not digging in. "I'm sorry, I'm just tired."

"That's ok, we don't have to talk."

Greer nodded.

Ceiley thought of her mother, baking pie this very minute. Letting her go just a little more each day. She looked at Greer who no longer had anyone—neither to look after nor to look after him. Miss Elizabeth had been so frail, but she had been his only family. Ceiley wondered if Greer would stay in Bannen. Did he consider this home?

Her eyes pricked again and this time she couldn't blame it on the food or the hot pepper. "You're not alone," she said quietly. "We're just across the street."

Greer looked up, his own eyes glistening. He nodded again. "Thank you, Ceiley. That means a lot."

They ate the rest of the meal in silence, Ceiley doing what she hadn't done in a long time—at least not for real. Pray, as her mother would have her pray. For Greer, for herself, and for her mother, too. She found herself thanking her lucky stars she still had Esse. And 'love thy neighbor?' That made sense.

When there was a knock at the door, both she and Greer were startled by the noise, but then they got up to let Esse in. She carried a blueberry pie and had brought whipped cream, too. They all enjoyed it, ready for something sweet.

FIFTEEN

(1977)

G reer, who'd never felt he belonged anywhere, was amazed at how many people came to pay their respects. Everyone in East Bannen. It didn't matter that Elizabeth had mostly kept to herself; she was one of them. Was he, too?

In those next few days, Esse brought over more than marinated chicken or her green bean casserole—she made every meal. Sometimes Ceiley would bring the food while her mother continued cooking. She'd set the pot on the kitchen table, silently take off the tin foil if it was time to eat. She'd place the food in front of him, didn't try to talk unless it seemed he wanted to, but sat with him in a quiet dignity to keep him company. Greer tried not to question what he'd done to deserve such care. Gratitude. He was trying to learn gratitude.

With Reverend Smith he went over the details of the service. He wondered, in a passing thought, whether Elizabeth was even allowed in the church, she who had renounced it long ago. The Reverend put to rest any such concerns: "Elizabeth was a child of God," he said without prompting. "She's returned home."

The Reverend had graying hair around the temples, a vein that pulsed there, too. The whites of his eyes were red, as if he'd been crying for many days. Greer noticed these things as they sat in the living room, talking over which passages to read. The minister had many suggestions. He could say that was just his job, but Greer sensed something else. People mean more to each other than they often let on. The things we carry, Greer thought. It's not always clear who's haunting whom.

Several times, Greer tried to write something himself. He was to speak after Reverend Smith. He searched, but no book, no poem, expressed what he should say. Only he had the words this time. No one else could do it for him.

When he was called to give his eulogy, in that humble church packed to the brim, he walked slowly to the podium, placed a hand on each side. He looked out at all those faces turned up towards him. These people held no ill will, he thought. They might think him strange, a stranger, as he himself felt, but they came in respect.

"I used to think my mother was weak," he said. "So quiet. Fragile. Sad. This is what I always thought when I was growing up. And even when I came back just a few short months ago."

He had no speech, nothing written down.

"I didn't realize how strong she was." He looked out at the people waiting. He was waiting, too. What was he waiting for? "I've spent years on my own," he said. "I've tried never to rely on anyone else. I thought, it's no great victory to make it on one's own. I've done it. I don't deserve a medal for that." He paused. "But why didn't I think about it, what it takes to raise a child? She wasn't alone. She had me. And I always had everything I needed."

The church was silent. He gripped the podium. The floor underneath him creaked as he shifted his weight.

"I've been searching for a lot of things. Trying to understand, searching for grace. I thought for a long time she didn't want me. That I was a mistake. Then I just carried on making mistakes. But you know what? She chose me. She had to sacrifice certain things for me and I never gave her credit for that. I was always searching for the other part of myself. That I didn't look at who was before me the whole time."

Greer looked at the coffin. He had asked for a closed casket; he didn't want to see that skeletal figure again. They had told him, he would see—with the embalming fluid and makeup, she would look as he remembered. But he kept it shut. Physical reminders weren't necessary; memory and deed were the most potent forces of all.

"She battled the hell out of this cancer. She wasn't even going to give it a name. What I took as weakness was not that at all. What we think we know, what we think we see, it's not that at all."

Greer pulled a handkerchief from his pocket and wiped his brow.

"I'm sorry, Mama. You were right there the whole time and I didn't see."

Greer hadn't realized, but he had closed his eyes. He opened them again, and saw a hundred faces looking at him with a mix of expressions—curiosity, confusion, compassion. Esse and Ceiley, sitting close in the front pew, looked especially touched.

"I'm not a religious man," Greer said. "But I'm going to do something like pray now. I'd ask you to pray, too, those who knew her. That things are easier on the other side for her. That she gets to sing. That somehow she can hear my voice now and know that I loved her."

"We'll pray with you," Wilson called out.

"I wasn't easy, but I'm learning about love."

"Praise be," someone else said.

"I'm trying. I never told her."

"Go on."

"I know what you did for me. I love you, Mama."

Soon many voices called out, "Amen."

He sat back down with the rest of the congregation. Esse nodded, then gave him a reassuring squeeze. "Brother Greer."

*   *   *

There was a nip in the air, fall coming soon. A good suit kept off the chill, but some of the women looked cold. Earlier in the day, the black fabric of their dresses had absorbed the sun's warmth, but now the waning afternoon's rays were weak. They held little heat. Those who had them placed sweaters over shoulders, walked close to loved ones. They made their way to the cemetery in silence.

Greer couldn't have known it would be looking into that hole in the ground that would dig deepest into his heart. As Elizabeth's coffin was lowered, the chorus sang. There was no soloist, only a unison of voices, "I'll Fly Away" sung on high. Everything he had buried inside was coming alive. The pain, the years of struggle.

Her plot was located halfway up a small hill. People leaned into the incline. One by one, each person present bent down and picked up a handful of dirt, began to throw it on her casket. The soil's moisture depended on from how deep in the earth it had come.

"The Lord is my shepherd; I shall not want," the Reverend said.

Greer scooped up a large pile of dirt as if the quantity could somehow express what he was feeling. He held it in his right hand, the soil cool to the touch.

"He maketh me to lie down in green pastures; He leadeth me beside the still waters…"

Greer felt the weight of the earth in his palm. He thought of his mother's fear of water, how she was being returned to dry land. He thought of his own years on the sea, running away from everything here. He thought about how he had forgotten nothing. Bannen was in his blood.

"… Yea, though I walk through the valley of the shadow of death, I will fear no evil…"

He spread his fingers, releasing the dirt. The wind blew it sideways before it fell.

"Rest in peace, Mama," he said. "I hope you find peace."

When the official rituals of death were finished, people gave their condolences in soft voices, knew enough to leave him there alone. Esse told him not to rush, to come when he was ready.

He stood looking into the grave for a long time. Dusk was falling; the sun would soon drop from the sky. The temperature had dropped, too. Even the pressure of the air felt different; it changed all at once.

A murder of crows shrieked above. Greer looked up. Why did those birds always gather in graveyards? Morbid messengers, outstretched wings. He watched them fly overhead, settle onto hanging tree limbs.

Then an engine's roar cut through the air. Greer turned in time to see a navy car crest the hill. It stopped at the peak.

Greer's blood went cold. No one in East Bannen had that car, nor would they drive here; it was so close to town. The thought that had hovered in the back of his mind since escaping Mrs. Thomas' house returned to the fore. That terrifying mob, the shouts, and the chase. He looked around, glanced at the cemetery gates.

The air hung taut, the sky crowding in. Simply dusk descending or the darkening before rain?

The car door opened. Greer started backing up.

A cane hit the ground, then a slim leg. Then a lone feminine figure got out.

Greer was surprised. Waited. No one else emerged.

From this distance he couldn't tell much: a white woman in a black suit, a veil across her face. Was there some other funeral? No one else was around. She didn't seem to be there to pay private respects at any gravesite, either, as she stood still in place.

Greer stood still, too, the two of them like statues. The woman's energy seemed directed toward him. They both stayed that way, at attention, for what seemed like a long time. Finally the woman took a few steps toward him, so Greer stepped forward, too, started up the hill.

As he neared, the mysterious pull—invisible, magnetic, undeniable—grew stronger. Just as it always had.

When he reached her, he saw she wore sunglasses, too, her whole face obscured by the veil and the shades. He stood just below her, the incline making it hard to find even ground.

"Are you hurt?" He fought the impulse to reach out and touch her, wondered about the cane, whose silver handle glinted in the waning light.

"If we were just meeting for the first time, what do you think we'd say?" she asked. "Do you think we'd still say we were nobodies?"

Greer drew in a deep breath and shook his head. "No," he said. "We were never nobodies."

She didn't say anything. What did she see as she looked at him? Or was she surveying the expanse of tombs, the stone markers all around them? Her hidden expression created even greater unease. "Really something," she said finally. "I thought we could get away with anything."

Greer's lips stretched into a grim line. "We didn't, did we?"

"You didn't even give it a chance."

Greer's throat tightened. "What do you want me to say, Caroline?"

She didn't respond, and he thought he might go mad staring at the lace, the inscrutable mask. Then, as if she had read his mind, and maybe she had, she took off her shades, which lifted the veil. Revealed her face. It was just as striking, more elegant, untouched. Save the lines life gives us for living. Her eyes, the blue still pierced, but there was a vulnerability there, which he hadn't heard in her voice.

"Mama said you came looking for me. What were you going to say?"

The horrible scene on Mrs. Thomas' doorstep flashed through his mind again. But she must not have told those men where to find him. She had told Caroline instead.

Greer looked in her eyes, though it was strained and hard, his stomach clenched like a fist. "I'm sorry," he said. "For everything."

Caroline's face didn't change. She held his gaze for what felt like a long time. Then she looked away for a second, before turning back. "You have no idea."

Greer exhaled. He hadn't realized he'd been holding his breath. "No," he said. "But some."

They stood there, silent. Their shadows stretched longer and longer across the grass.

"I was so angry at you," she said. "For so many years."

Greer dropped his chin. The elongating shadows threatened to blot out all remaining light.

Caroline's voice was steady, her voice so calm. "But I've had a long time to think it over. I knew before you did, Greer."

He cocked his head slightly as if he couldn't hear. "What?" he said.

"Right before you left. I figured it out. But by then it didn't change how I felt."

Greer drew back a little as if to create more space for this new revelation. New betrayal?

"I don't understand."

Caroline sighed, a sound heavy with regret. "We thought we were so different from our parents, didn't we? All those secrets. But we did the same thing."

His brow furrowed. "Why didn't you tell me?"

"Why didn't you?" she fired back.

Greer, still dumb, had no reply. More shocking information someone close to him had hidden. Another disclosure that would have changed his life.

Caroline looked out wistfully, as if beyond the cemetery, the ground just virgin land. "From the beginning, I felt a deep connection. Deeper than I'd ever felt."

Greer nodded his head, then shook it, the contradictory emotions animating his body, his soul, in strange ways. Confused as he had been, he had thought he was protecting her in some way, hadn't he? Maintaining her innocence, walking away with the burden. But what was innocence in this case? "We were so young," he whispered.

"What happens when you're young stays with you forever," she said.

Greer found it hard to breathe, to swallow. "But how could you live with it?"

Caroline let out a sad exhale and shook her head. "It was never our fault to love."

The evening's chill drummed forward, a soft wind blowing. Was a storm still coming? Shadows now stretched all the way from the top of the hill down to the valley. The words hung in the air, long enough to take their measure, test their weight. It struck him quietly, as the big truths usually do. He closed his eyes and felt the pressure pounding. He opened them again and saw Caroline, mermaid, real, swimming before his eyes.

"You left me alone to deal with everything," she said, starting to cry, too.

Water leaked down Greer's face, but he didn't make a sound. Some pain dwelled so deep inside that only silence reverberated there. He felt Caroline encircle him with her arms. He remained stiff at first, but finally relented, buried himself against her chest. The warmth there repelled the cold night, made it disappear. He could feel the rapidly beating heart, though whether it was his or hers, he couldn't tell, didn't care.

"I'm here now," he said.

SIXTEEN

(1977)

There'd never been so much activity. Even after this many hours' wait, when some had already slipped away, unsure whether Brother Greer wanted them to stay, the noise of dozens of neighbors packed into Elizabeth's house spilled out onto the street, voices rising and falling. The idea of a party directly on the heels of death always seemed a little odd to Greer, but it felt good somehow to spy the house so animated, something it had never experienced before.

He and Caroline had continued their conversation until the cemetery gates closed, Caroline tapping the earth with her walking stick, a formal accessory only now, though for a time she'd needed it. She'd been in a car accident soon after he left.

"I was so reckless." She looked at him gravely. "I didn't realize how much danger I had put you in back then, too."

Now Caroline carefully pulled her car up to the front of his house, then shifted to park. She studied the modest structure, dignified despite a wobbly railing, a sloping roof, minimalist and self-contained. Greer followed her eyes. It occurred to him she'd never seen where he was raised.

As they made their way to the doorstep, they could hear his childhood home alive with his mother's wake. But when he and Caroline opened the door, all the sound stopped. The pleasant murmur they'd heard on the porch transformed into a vibrating hush. All the faces turned toward them. Everyone stared. The longcase clock ticked in the hallway. No one said a thing.

He and Caroline stood there for a moment, then slowly stepped inside. People parted the way for them in almost ceremonial fashion. But the unspoken question buzzed, electrifying the room's very air.

"Family," Greer said finally as explanation.

Those who remembered their manners didn't let it show on their faces. Those who didn't couldn't keep their expressions in check.

"Well go on now," Wilson said, finally breaking the silence. "Family's family."

There were a few "mmm-hmmms," but the room remained quiet. No matter—people would have plenty to say later. *Always knew he must have white blood. But family? What kind of kin was she?*

There was no getting back on track after that, even though some pretended. People milled around a little longer hoping to learn more juice, but when it became clear they wouldn't be getting any right then, they began to leave in small clusters. They could feel the frequency between these two, serious business. "Brother Greer," they said, offering last condolences. "Ma'am," they nodded at Caroline, self-conscious and strained.

Greer caught Ceiley's eye. She'd been watching them raptly, like everyone else. But she wasn't judging, just marveling again at how many surprises he'd brought into town. He nodded at her and she nodded back, not sure of the situation, but somehow seeming to gain in size.

He looked at Esse, her arm wrapped around Ceiley, and a warmth flooded his chest. He thought he understood now. He lived it, too. That we tell ourselves what we need to in order to get through. Just one story, we can let it define our whole life. But should we?

When he and Caroline were alone again, they could continue with the impossible task: trying to catch up on sixteen years, explain it all in one night.

But they seemed in silent agreement that they'd already said enough for one day.

"May I?" Caroline asked, her hand hovering near the lamp closest to the couch. "My eyes are so tired."

Greer assented.

She turned off the light, leaving the room dim. Softer.

He sank into his mother's big chair across from the sofa. He looked around, spotting evidence of the lively scene that must have been here earlier: plates with picked-over food, empty beer cans and wine bottles. Plenty of spirits, too. He imagined the genial gossip that must have flowed through the room. A fine repast.

"I'm sorry about your mother, Greer," Caroline said, bringing him back.

He nodded.

"Truly," she said. Her voice dropped lower. "I'm sorry for everything."

Greer didn't respond right away. He thought over all that had happened just today—and the many layers of truth. "I know," he said quietly. He got up and walked to the window. He looked out. East Bannen was quiet again, no one on the street.

Caroline came to join him. She placed her hand briefly on the glass as she peered up at the sky. "Looks like that storm didn't come after all."

Greer raised his gaze and agreed. Cricketsong and other eventide ballads seeped through the pane. Neither said anything for a long time.

"Remember that game we used to play?" Caroline said.

"Where we'd pick a new place to travel each day?"

She gave a small smile. "Paris, Hong Kong…"

His lips edged slightly upward, too, but his gaze stayed fixed out the window. "I made it to some of those places, you know."

"Oh?" she said. "I hope you'll tell me about them sometime."

He didn't say anything for awhile.

"It's good I came home," he said finally. "If only to move on."

Caroline barely moved, but after a moment, she slowly nodded her head. "You're the only reason I could even bring myself to come back here," she said, her voice shaky. "It's been good to see you, Greer."

He felt a lump in his throat, making it hard to speak.

"It's not true what they say," he managed.

"What's that?"

"The grass isn't always greener on the other side. At least, it can't be, if you're just running. You leave things behind."

He turned to her then, the air inside still and close. He slowly extended his hand. The weak glow from the porch light caught her eyes as they started to glisten. She reached out her hand to meet his. They looked at each other and held on for a long time. Then they turned to the window again. Stood side by side and said nothing. Stared straight ahead.

Outside different sounds filled a night that had finally swallowed up all traces of day, turned off the sun. Snake Creek was dark, except for tiny flashes of moon and starlight that caught the water and set it shining. The woods were thick as ever, forest life scurrying in the underbrush, other animals going to sleep, not a person for miles around.

In the cemetery, two workers whistled, took their time. Lamps cast light and shadow across their bent backs, light and dark both while they hummed. Large heaps of Bannen soil rained down on the casket, filled in Elizabeth's grave. The open ground slowly rose to meet the sky. Shovels packed the dirt down after, made it level as a plain.

ACKNOWLEDGMENTS

When the time between first page written to published book in hand spans more than a dozen years, it can be hard to account for all the generous people who have helped bring this novel to life. From close confidantes to strangers offering serendipitous inspiration, so many have played a part. Thank you to publisher Elizabeth Earley and the entire Jaded Ibis Press team for ushering *As a River* into the world. I'm indebted to Rosalie Morales Kearns who connected us; she has been a guardian angel for this book and continues to champion it.

Thanks to Sarah Van Arsdale who witnessed the full journey, from conception to completion. I workshopped the novel's very beginnings – back when I thought it was a short story – in her cozy NYC living room. Years later my kind mentor has become a cherished friend.

Sarah also led me to other mentors, most notably by suggesting an MFA at Vermont College of Fine Arts where the bulk of this book was written. There I studied with fantastic faculty including Domenic Stansberry, Xu Xi, Connie May Fowler, and Robert Vivian. Ellen Lesser and Clint McCown played particularly large roles in helping me create and shape the manuscript. I came to them with fragments and they showed me how to start stringing them together into a whole.

I had several beta readers whose opinions were invaluable: Elena Azzoni, Karin Lynn Bates, Kerry Breen, Ayako Harvie Buliard, Sonya Chung, Danya Dayson, Jennifer Geraghty, Kaaren Kitchell, Devin McKinney, Jodi Paloni, Edward Smallfield, Michal Tal, Melanie Vaz. Sophie Hardach's suggestion to imagine the different time periods as narrative washing lines helped immensely in revision.

Julie Christine Johnson, Abbey Keith, Anna Polonyi, and Angela Watrous were excellent readers late in the process during a crisis of faith. Some last-minute counsel by Naomi J. Williams helped me over the finish line.

A special shout-out goes to Emily Monaco who read countless versions and was always available to help me sort through all level of concerns with her incredible insight and grace. I can't wait to see her beautiful book(s) out in the world, too.

Thanks to Juliet Oppong-Asare of the University of Cape Coast and Paa Kojo Winful for assistance with the Ghanaian material.

Gratitude to Kasia Ozga for the use of an image from her powerful series "Internal Frontier" for the cover art.

Throughout the book I've quoted lines from poetry in the public domain. Wherever possible I've named the poet in the scene. On page 72 the quote is by Lord Byron; page 91, William Wordsworth. Praise to poetry that has saved me many a time.

I'm thankful for a grant from the Money for Women/ Barbara Deming Memorial Fund, a residency at the Kerouac House, and a Callaloo Creative Writing Workshop led by Ravi Howard for support in writing this book.

Thanks to my mom. For everything. To my dad, for believing I could do anything. To Frédéric Monpierre, my rock during so much of this process. To my friends – my chosen family.

Home is in the people you love.